DOUBLE BARREL

NICOLAS FREELING

DOUBLE

BARREL

VINTAGE BOOKS
A Division of Random House
New York

First Vintage Books Edition, March 1981
Copyright © 1964 by Nicolas Freeling
All rights reserved under International and Pan-
American Copyright Conventions. Published in
the United States by Random House, Inc., New
York. Originally published by Harper & Row,
Publishers, New York, in 1964.

Library of Congress Cataloging in Publication Data
Freeling, Nicolas.
Double barrel.
Reprint of the 1st ed. published in 1965 by
Harper & Row, New York.
I. Title.
[PR6056.R4D6 1981] 823′.914 80-6128
ISBN 0-394-74693-7

Manufactured in the United States of America

DOUBLE BARREL

PART ONE

HAPPENSTANCE

1

How OFTEN DOESN'T it happen? We imagine some situation, or even construct a whole hypothetical case in the course of a discussion. It may be serious; it may be said just as a joke. But the next week it comes true. There is something laughable about it even when the reality is disagreeable.

Back in his office, Van der Valk did laugh, but the irreverence might have been to offset a strong idea that the next few weeks would be unpleasant. It was ridiculous, and from this far away it was fairly funny—but it was sinister, it was horrible, and it was certainly tragic.

There it was. He had gone and theorized, all pompously. And today his hypothesis was presented to him complete in every detail.

A lot of good his theorizing would do him now. As likely as not, he was going to fall straight on his classic scornful nose.

It was his wife's fault. He wasn't unhappy that Arlette was French; it had helped him often enough to
remember not to be quite so Dutch when he tried to
understand things. After twelve years she was still rebellious about Holland, and sometimes uneasy there.
She wouldn't surrender to some of the attitudes natural
to any Dutch woman, with the generations behind
them of what she called their conditioned reflex. It
sounded like Mr. Pavlov's dogs, and there was a good
deal in common there.

It had been not even a week ago, in the evening.
She was reading the paper and he was sitting in his
socks, majestically doing nothing, probably with the
socks on the coffee table where he could admire
their intricate beauty; gray wool, ninety-eight cents in
the January sales that were just over. The wall of
newsprint opposite gave an indignant crackle. A voice
said "Pah!"

"What is pah?" No great interest; just making a
sympathetic sound.

"An advertisement for soap powder. In a headline,
sub-heading, and five lines of text, the word 'Fresh'
is repeated six times. S-I-X."

"Ach. Every time they want to sell something to a
housewife, they tell her how fresh it will make her
gray existence."

"But six times . . ."

"It's a witch word. Everything approved of in Holland is fresh, whether it's the kitchen floor or a pretty
girl."

Snort from Arlette.

"I only buy things from now on that are unfresh."

"Ha. I read a film review the other day; the sort of

film—you know, takes the lid off the call-girl industry. Described by the reviewer as 'decidedly unfresh'— you could see him holding his nose."

"I wish to go and see it immediately."

"I wonder what he'd call my daily life."

"Not as fresh as we would like."

He got an idea, with a mild galvanic effect aiming his feet toward the bookshelf. A book he had annotated. The annotations were probably silly, but he thought about Louis XVIII, writing little notes in the margin of his Horace while Napoleon was on his way from Elba. Van der Valk being civilized while Amsterdam wallows in unfresh crime. Poor fellow; he's tired.

"You don't understand Holland. Listen—this is Stendhal, talking about the America of 1820. Meaning Puritan New England, over a hundred years after the Salem witch trials. Where am I? Yes—'The physical gaiety of Americans disappears as they reach twenty. A habit of reason, of caution, of prudence, makes love impossible.' What does that remind you of? He cites, by the way, a mental climate hostile to art or literature."

"It does sound like Holland."

"Or this—describing a love affair in Protestant North Germany. 'The sun is pale in Halberstadt, the government very particular, and these two personages pretty cold. In the most passionate tête-à-tête, Kant and Klopstock are always present.' "

"Giggle as you like—I don't think it's funny."

"Be glad you live in Amsterdam. Think of living in a provincial town in Drente, and discovering that

murder was a crime, right enough, but that falling
asleep during the sermon was a lot worse."

"Is that the worst crime?"

"I think that making love to your wife in the living
room in the middle of the afternoon would count as
the most serious."

2

He was in the office on the Marnixstraat next morning, unraveling a long wearisome report about a bank
fraud. Holland is a strange country. Every single
thing is fragmented, organized, and subject to a
thick book of rules, and here was the treasurer of a
large concern happily speculating with thousands
that weren't his—undetected, not even suspected for
years. He looked, you see, so utterly respectable, and
the rules were such gobbledygook that nobody could
understand them anyway without three hard-earned
diplomas. The phone buzzed. Van der Valk's superior,
Commissaris Tak of Central Recherche. An old maid
if ever there was one.

"Van der Valk? The Procureur-Général wants to
see you. Right away."

"Oh Lord, what have I done wrong now?"

"Nothing, as far as I know."

"What's it about?"

"I haven't been told. You'd better get over to the
Prinsengracht and find out, hadn't you?"

He put his jacket on. Central heating was too hot
today. Real February; westerly, windy, rainy. Not cold,
but here that did not mean that winter was over. It'd
probably be snowing tomorrow.

"Nice and fresh," his colleague had said, coming in that morning. They shared a room; there was space for the two of them, their papers, and maybe one beer bottle carefully concealed behind a report on the number of auto thefts in 1938.

It is five minutes' walk to the Palace of Justice, and Van der Valk spent it wondering what he would be told off for. The Procureur-Général was a most important personage. He was supposed to be busy presenting appeal cases to the Court of Cassaton, or codifying public morals, but he had a trick of finding time to censure imprudence of unimportant functionaries— and that had meant Van der Valk more than once.

There is a barrier to penetrate of pale legal advisers before one reaches the sanctuary where the big Boums contemplate pale legal paper in utter silence. Here the telephone lines are all guarded, and probably the lowest typist is under some awe-filling oath—Safety of the Realm Act 1823.

At least in the other half of this big building it is more human. There sits the Parquet—the prosecutors, the Officers of Justice, and the Children's Court— and policemen sit on benches with criminals in an atmosphere of almost cordiality. Over here, the milk of human kindness has been in the autoclave. Well and truly sterile.

He reached a secretary, an elderly soul with prim blue hair and no lips.

"Inspector van der Valk, on the instructions of Commissaris Tak."

An approving nod for that. She picked up the intercom phone and spoke in hushed tones. The Vatican voice—Cardinal commanding the Holy Office, speaking.

"Will you please go straight in?"

Master Anthoni Sailer, learned in the law, was a tall dry man, a bit creaky. Body, nose, lip—all long and perfectly straight. The straight hair combed across a high white forehead to hide a balding patch was still dark. His look was direct—yes, straight. And his handwriting was upright and always legible, in black ink with a fine pen. But he was capable of understanding. Even, as Van der Valk once learned during an otherwise unpleasant interview, capable of humor. Acid, arid, but humor.

"Ah—Van der Valk. Sit down, then." He took a horizon-blue folder from the side of his desk, opened it, arranged it perfectly parallel to the edge of his blotter, and studied the opening paragraph of the contents. A short pause, legal but pregnant, gave Van der Valk time to wonder what it contained.

"I have been posed an unusual problem, and after thought I have reached an unusual conclusion. Incidentally, have you ever been in Drente?"

"No, sir."

"I am thinking of sending you there."

Big fright. He had a sudden vision of Louis XV saying in his icy voice, "M. Maurepas, you will retire immediately to your estate in the country." Damn it, I'll resign first.

"It would amount to a temporary detachment, upon a temporary duty. An unusual duty, and delicate. Demanding tact as well as ability. Naturally, you may refuse if you wish; it is not an order. But first you must study this folder."

Leisurely, Master Sailer drew a little tube of throat lozenges from his breast pocket and popped one with dignity behind his wisdom tooth. There was a minute twitch, but not by a millimeter did it bulge the straight shaved cheek.

"I have upon occasion"—slowly—"criticized your handling of circumstances. And I have had occasion to praise your—penetration. Since this affair calls for just that quality, I am asking you to use it—but with more discretion than you have been known to show."

"Thank you, sir."

"I thought of you, among the officers of police within my jurisdiction."

"Thank you, sir."

"You would have, consequently, the complete confidence and support of the relevant authorities. Possessing that confidence, that support, you are capable of justifying my choice. As I estimate."

"Thank you, sir."

"Good. Drente, you are doubtless thinking, is not within my jurisdiction. This problem is now over six months old. It has baffled—the word is not too strong —the local municipal police of a small town called Zwinderen, an inspector from Assen, and has subsequently become the subject of inquiry by the State Recherche officers, who have produced a file of exhaustive investigation with little positive result. The file finally reached my colleague in Leeuwarden, who has sent it to me for study and possible comment. His conclusion was that a man from the city—with, that is to say, no local connections or even knowledge— may overcome the apparent obstacles. I am prepared,

conditional to your acceptance, to advise him that you
may be the man for this task."

What answer could one make to that?

"I will now give you the relevant parts of this dossier for study."

"Can I take them home?"

"Files here don't get taken home. They get studied
here; they don't leave this building. There is a small
room where you will be undisturbed. Take the whole
morning if you wish. I shall inform Mr. Tak that I am
holding you at my disposal. Come back when you
have decided. You will have to consider whether you
believe yourself competent to succeed where these
other gentlemen"—with a sudden gleam—"got stuck
in the bog."

All Van der Valk knew about Drente was that it was
up in the northeast corner of Holland, between Groning-
en and the German border. A poor province, the
ground is not much good for agriculture. Wet, peaty
sort of moorland. What in Ireland is called the bog.
Oh.

It had taken him nearly five minutes to see that
Sailer had made a joke.

Rather flabbergasted, he was led to a small menacing room, and the photostat girl brought him a cup of
legal coffee. After reading the first twenty pages of
general introductory remarks, he gave a sort of moan.
Why hadn't Arlette kept her mouth shut?

Twenty pages further he was thinking that this affair was a bit unfresh, too. And that, doubtless, was
why everybody seemed to have thought of Van der
Valk.

3

"Well?"

"Well, sir—I mean yes, sir. I accept, of course. May I state a few brief conclusions, or shall I say a few steps that I think it would be necessary to take?"

"Certainly."

"There's been a lot of policemen. One move, and he won't get anywhere at all—more likely to get his eye blackened. I believe, sir, that if I go at all it should not be as a policeman. Am I allowed to make a suggestion?"

"Yes."

"A state functionary, with some foolproof cover to explain the nosing about and questioning. A—a—I don't know—an inspector of tax dividends or something. I think that nobody should know who or what I am."

Thought. Doubt. Reconsideration. Conclusion.

"The point is well taken. The burgomaster will have to know. You will be responsible to him—but to him alone—and can make a direct verbal report. But this —cover—I think I can agree and I think I could arrange it." A weird but indubitably legal smile. "How would you like to be an official—a responsible official —of the Ministry of the Interior? That is not, technically, an untruth. Shall we say that such an official might be sent from The Hague to draw up a detailed report on aspects of a provincial town? Perhaps with a view to the further industrial expansion in a district of underdevelopment? Mm. Your powers of inquiry should be very broad and extremely vague. I am

casting about for a suitably vague, impressive, minatory phrase. . . . Suppose we were to say that you were
conducting ethnographic research? That means nothing
and will cover everything."

Really, Van der Valk thought, he has understood; I
have to be able to blind the tiny local bigwigs with
bullshit.

"I dislike conspiracies, but this is an unorthodox
situation. It is justifiable to meet it in an unorthodox
way." Meditating. "I have no doubt but that you can
be provided with a lodging, transport, an identity, as
well as various necessary papers." Very cool indeed.

He reached for the private-line telephone.

"Will you please get me the Minister of the Interior
in The Hague?"

"There is a further point," he said while his call was
winging toward another discreet burr in another
padded paneled office. "I should like you to be accompanied by your wife. You may be there some time,
and if you are to be the complete convincing, colorless,
though intelligent state functionary, you need a wife
to do the housekeeping."

"My wife is French, sir."

"Better a French wife than none at all," remarked
Mr. Sailer charmingly.

"Ah, good morning, Excellency. . . ."

4

A week later Van der Valk had a black Volkswagen
and a new identity supported by most impressive and
not quite totally incomprehensible papers. He was
making a preliminary survey of Zwinderen, a small

market town rapidly growing past the fifteen-thousand mark, in the extreme northeastern corner of the province of Drente, a scant thirty-five miles from the German border. As an official introduction to this new sphere, he had an appointment with the burgomaster.

A modern town hall, very large for a place this size. Very ugly for anywhere. Lot of money and all wasted. The steps were very grand, where the couples stand to be photographed after being married, the farmers' sons vastly uneasy in hired top hats. You don't even get married by the mayor with his scarf on in Holland. A character does it whose title is Functionary of the Civil Status; there's nothing more Dutch than that. The steps of the town hall have to be pretty grand to make up for it. But Holland can be nice. There are tiny dorps in Freisland that were places of importance in the sixteenth century, with perhaps five thousand souls now, but possessing magnificent Renaissance and baroque town halls, their façades towering and curling above sleepy tiny squares, and steps . . . like Napoleon taking leave of the Old Guard, at Fontainebleau.

Inside, black-and-white rubber marble. Aseptic corridors, with glass sliding windows to protect the functionary from the contagious coughing public. Various depressed members of said public, waiting to be noticed and kindly to be allowed to register a child's birth—but only if the name is approved of by the *Handbook for Functionaries of the Civil Status*. And finally a light, airy, freshly painted office. The burgomaster got up from his desk when a neat and competent-seeming female showed Van der Valk in.

He had a firm, resilient face; quite the portrait of a burgomaster. He could hang later in some pompous frame, looking down benignly on the couples getting married. Not quite on the same wall as the swimmy-sentimental portraits of royalty, but well up there in the league—presented by a grateful municipality after he retired, handsome and silver-haired. But he did not look a nonentity. Van der Valk had already decided that he would not be a dud; this was the man in charge of a town scheduled for expansion to a thriving industrial community. In twenty years there would be sixty thousand people here; it was already well on the way and it was his work.

"Good morning, burgomaster."

"Good morning. Pleased to make your acquaintance." He turned to the secretary, waiting with an alert, impersonal face. "Accessible to no one. I am in conference."

"Very good, burgomaster." The door shut crisply.

"I have an hour. Sit down, Mr. van der Valk. Let us get to know each other—and see what we can do for each other."

An hour later Van der Valk had acquired a lot. Access to everything, neat dockets of disturbing information in close detail, assurance of every cooperation, a hearty handshake, and a request for a verbal report twice a week at least—at his home; that would be more discreet. No need to let the municipal officials into our little secret. Van der Valk was an embarrassment; the burgomaster would prefer to see as little as possible of him officially. He could see how the burgomaster disliked this hole-and-corner game, but he had been convinced of its necessity.

Van der Valk got passed to the secretary, who was helpful. He had been wondering where on earth he

was going to be lodged, and what the point of the wife
was. Now he found that the wheels had turned, and
the hand of the Procureur-Général had reached as
far as this tiny tentacle of central government.

"I have been instructed, Mr. Van der Valk"—
bright, very efficient, and both conscious and proud of
it—"that you will be staying here a few weeks. You'll
be glad to hear that I've a furnished house for you—
oh, only a little one, but at least you'll be independent
of hotels. You see, we do quite often have to house
officials—inspectors, headmasters, people whose own
houses and belongings aren't yet ready. Or of course
people who are here temporarily, as in your case.
We've had functionaries from The Hague before, doing
these administrative surveys. I'm afraid the furniture
is rather nondescript but it's adequate. The house
does tend to look as though it had no owner. Well, of
course, it hasn't. I do hope your wife will be comfortable—but if there's any little thing you or
she needs, you've only to ask me. Any help—I'm delighted if I can be of service."

Simple as that. In another week, he would be in-
stalled, with Arlette and several suitcases, in the
Mimosastraat in Zwinderen, province of Drente. With
access to everything. He had already arranged for the
children to be boarded out, in the house of Inspector
and Mrs. Suykerland of the Amsterdam Police. They
would get frightful food, but they were delighted with
the notion. It all sounded like a holiday. All he had to
do was clear up an affair that had not only baffled
a lot of people just as intelligent as he but that had
also been trodden on by so many big boots full of flat
feet as to be nearly illegible.

5

He had already been relieved of all ordinary duties;
Mr. Tak was irritated but floored by a minatory letter
from the Prinsengracht. By the time they moved, Van
der Valk had spent six days studying—but on paper,
only on paper—the life of Zwinderen, which, when he
had gone to school, had been an ossified tiny market
town away in the wilds, a stone's throw from Protestant North Germany. But now it had become the frontier of the big push at decentralization, decongestion,
full employment, and Prosperity for All. A boom town.
Light industry and housing. Practically Dodge City.
He was Wyatt Earp, getting sent there as United
States Marshal. He had better start polishing his forty-
five and practicing quick draws.

The key word in this northeastern corner of Holland
is "Veen." It occurs as a suffix in place names. Over
to the west are Hoogeveen and Heerenveen—larger
towns these, around the twenty-thousand mark. To
the south Klazinaveen, Vriezenveen—smaller, hardly
more than villages. The second word is "Kanaal,"
which means, mostly, a ditch. Stadskanaal, Mussel-
kanaal. "Veen" means "turf," the boggy, peaty moorland that was cut for fuel in the depression days, before
the oil pipelines and the natural gas. The canals drain
it—a network of tiny waterways. There are a great
many; this country takes a lot of draining. But there is
no watershed, and green scummy water dribbles
vaguely in all directions—toward the Ems estuary, and
down south toward rivers. The biggest of the canals

have some mercantile use, and there is quite a lot of plodding barge traffic even now.

The funny thing is that the country is on the verge of a big upheaval. They found a "bubble" of natural gas up here. To see what is about to happen, one need only look at Lacq, in France—and this bubble is ten times the size of Lacq's. Traditionally, though, it has always been a very poor and barren land. Very little use for agriculture, and none at all for anything else. Penniless. But the government has already altered all that.

Railways and roads; factories processing milk, scrap metal, paper. Big trucks with trailers boomed along broad highways; new diesel railway cars linked Groningen and Winschoten at one end of the province with Emmen and Coevorden at the other; there was a branch line to Assen, with connections to the main line south.

More sophisticated industry had been tempted into following. A small but enterprising firm built coach and even aircraft bodies; another, directed by a brilliant engineer, was internationally known for electronic equipment—"second Philips" was the local boast. A daughter firm of a huge combine was making wire and cable, and another forty-five per cent of the total Dutch output of heat-resistant glassware.

The sleepy little place hardly knew itself now.

Tiny shops, dark and smelly—corsets and cough mixture; wooden shoes and flat caps of gaudy cheap tweed; weed killer and sheep-dip; lumps of wet salt pork and margarine—were all airy and glassy now, with black and chromium fronts. Outside tumble-down farmhouses with sagging thatched roofs now stood tinny, brightly painted, brand-new autos. Behind the

main building soared concrete cowsheds and hay
barns, and fire-engine-colored tractors hauled the
swedes and the sugar beets in increasing masses at
greater speeds toward ever-greedier consumers.

Smelly canal backwaters, scummy green or inky
black, had been filled in, and the worn-out wood of
collapsing wharves was cleared up. Concrete came
pouring out of huge striped urns that revolved everywhere like merry-go-rounds; bright-pink brick streets
ate up the rutted car tracks. The workhouse-ward
schools were gone, and there was an annex to the hospital and even a swimming bath. True, the county insane asylum still stood gaunt in the sour fields; the
prunus and flowering-cherry trees were tiny and the
grass roadsides sickly; the few old stunted oaks
looked sad and lonely despite cheerful additions of
golden cypress and Montana pine.

But the bustle of the burgomaster—and generous
state funds—had infected the whole withered place
with new seeds and spores. Rebirth.

The local people, and with them a swelling tide of
strangers from congested metropolitan Holland, took
with enthusiasm to easy work in sunny canteen-and-
canned-music factories. A pleasant change from trying to dig a living out of wet black stinking ground.

The population had doubled and redoubled in ten
years, and now blocks of flats and streets of tiny bal-
conied brick houses—very Dutch, with extraordinarily
large windows—surrounded and hid the surviving
nineteenth-century cottages. But a few of the old
houses were still lived in, small, sad, depressing; witness still to the meanness, the bitterness, and the pa-
thos of life here for over a thousand years.

Van der Valk saw quite a lot of this the first visit. After the hour with the burgomaster, he spent the rest of the day strolling. Coffee in one café, a beer in another, and a greasy pork-chop lunch in the town's biggest, between a billiard table and six commercial travelers, all bolting their filthy chops with enthusiastic expense-account appetites.

It was wonderful winter weather, that first day. Windless, bright sun, and the canals frozen. The children stormed out of school, whooping, at four, and there instantly was the classic Dutch painting: a sun sinking redly behind the stepped gable and tiny spire of the Netherlands Reformed Church, and a thousand four-year-olds buttoned up to the eyes shrieking and tumbling on the old-fashioned long wooden skates. His eyes were on the houses, where the oblique beam of sun streamed in through a thousand enormous over-polished windows and lit up the interiors.

They looked like all the other Dutch interiors. Here a fat old coal stove, polished brilliant black, and the lumpy "gothic" wooden furniture upholstered in olive-green plush. There the streamlined gray oil burner, and "contemporary" mushrooms of chairs with knitting-needle legs and pink or mauve moquette. Either the old walnut-veneer dresser, with a tiny diamond-paned window showing souvenir German wineglasses (bulbous, green, with Loreleis painted on them) and turned chess-queen legs, or the flat slab of imitation teak. All proudly oiled and spotlessly dusted. Everywhere, of course, crammed with climbing plants, far too many lamps, and at least three too many tables. Since Pieter de Hooch, Dutch interiors have gone downhill.

None of this told him much about the people who
lived there. Were they, too, just like the ones in metroland? Had a thousand years in the "Veen" ground
produced a local type? There were local names; he
saw several "Van Veen" and "Van der Veen" name
plates on doors.

He found a local weekly paper to take home, seized
on it with joy. And once at home again, he nearly
wore it out. The cheap gray newsprint with its smudgy
blunt press frayed at the folds and then disintegrated
under the well-known heavy police hand and burning
police eye of our brilliant officer. It told him a lot.
Just for a start, births, deaths, and marriages. And—
a real invention of "the little province"—a careful
column telling one who has arrived in our midst, with
full details. Address he's come to, and come from. His
name and his profession. All compiled from the careful indexing and filing of our industriously nosy
functionaries in that damned town hall.

In these columns, one could spot the local people
easily. If Piet Jansen, the bricklayer from Zaandam,
had settled in the Dahliastraat, and Ria Bakker, the
secretary from Maassluis, was now filling the Widow
Pump's back room in the Vondelstraat, it was doubtless fascinating to their fellow locals.

The locals had ludicrous names. "Ook" and "Goop"
and "Unk." Their surnames were as bad, and there
were clans, of course—generations of intermarriage
no doubt.

"Cold Comfort Farm," said Arlette amusedly. "Seth
and Reuben, Dooms and Starkadders. No doubt
there'll be sukebind and water voles."

Quite right; no exaggeration whatever.

"And a lot of heavy-handed rural fornication in summer. *Rose Bernd* all over again."

He wasn't quite so sure about that one. The list of Sunday services in the paper was formidable. He counted carefully; there were seventeen different kind of churches.

The obvious ones first, of course. Netherlands Renewed Protestants. Even more Netherlands Reformed. A march of well-known "chapel" sects; Baptists and Methodists, Unitarians and Congregationalists. The rather queer ones, not quite certain of acceptance outside a well-tried little clique—Jehovah's Witnesses, Christian Scientists, Roman Catholics (oh, yes, definitely queer here).

But what was one to say to the wilder Irvingite and Campbellite aberrations that flourished in holy righteousness? Remonstrant Early Lutherans, Purged Presbyterians, Rigid Plymouth Brethren? Sects that didn't have churches; churches were neither rigid enough nor purged enough. They had Meeting Places of God's Elect. All that was lacking was Aimee Semple McPherson. It was a list to make Elmer Gantry lick his lips in holy joy and clap his great pious meaty hands together and uplift his voice in vociferous sanctity.

"No Jews or Quakers," remarked Arlette with interest.

"Plenty of by-Our-Lady hornyhanded early Christians, though—very early. Deacon Urk, Gravedigger Bloop, and Sexton Moogie, gathered around Dominie Prophecies-of-Malachi Thunk; she-that-commits it-shall-be-cut-off."

"Have a look," said Arlette. "Klaas Kip married Wilhelmina Dina Regina Vos."

"You haven't seen anything yet. You haven't read the report of the monthly meeting and tea drinking of the Rural Christian Women. Carry Nation presided at the bun fight. Takes one back a hundred years. Small towns in Iowa and South Dakota were like this in Elmer Gantry's extreme youth."

The happenings in this remote, comic place, where a sham modernism hid but did not alter knotted, rooted survivals, were as ludicrous as the names.

He was reminded of two things when he read the dossier first, and they never quite left him throughout the time he was there.

The first was easy, an obvious one. The Staphorst affair. The international press had picked it up as an example of primitive survivals in a modern world. Staphorst is a village in Drente, too, albeit the other end of the province. It has a closed little community and a sort of rural Calvinism unequaled for hell-fire savagery. They go to church in procession on Sundays, with downcast eyes and clasped Bibles, and the men have been known to break the cameras of gawking tourists. A pair there had been caught in adultery, had been—by report, among other things—drawn through the village in a cart and pelted.

The other memory was of a French film based on the classic case of the witches of Salem. Reading the dossier, Van der Valk had thought that twentieth-century Zwinderen had a good deal in common with seventeenth-century Massachusetts. Not only the pillory and the stocks, but the stake and the noose were not very far away.

Not so very much had happened, factually, and yet one could understand why the Procureur-Général in Leeuwarden and his colleague in Amsterdam had taken this so seriously. Two women had committed suicide, and a third had had to be led gently away by men in white coats. There had been an outbreak of anonymous letters—a blackmailing poison pen—and nobody knew how many of these had not come to light.

That was not so very much. But there was more, intangible but perceptible. Like Salem, the whole place sounded hysterical, neurotic. Neighborhood squabbles tended to be started by virtuous housewives, shrilly accusing other virtuous housewives of immorality. There were many, and they were too much alike.

There was a lot of immorality—a bit too much. He had the file on the past year's police-court cases heard behind locked doors. Incest, mm—never quite unknown in these ingrown intermarried districts. But rather too much rape, indecent exposure, dissemination of pornography, obscene dancing in cafés, underhand prostitution; beneath all the drumbeating and bell ringing on Sundays there was a sort of sexy itch. One could not get at it properly. Not only were the reports in a language so stilted, so proper, and so bureaucratic that he could hardly understand them himself, practiced as he was, but the witnesses were excessively hangdog and evasive—not to speak of the existence of wholesale perjury, obvious if quite unprovable.

One knows what "He then attempted to commit an offense" means, but one cannot cross-examine a nine-year-old girl in court after a respectable fifty-eight-

year-old farmer has been caught by his wife pulling
the child's pants off in a hayloft. He said things. What?
The child couldn't say and the wife wouldn't.

The letter writing. Something was common knowledge; other things had been debated in secret but were
subject to leakage. Some things were dead secret—
they said.

Neither the municipal police—always stilted in
language—nor the State Recherche—unembarrassed,
flowery, practiced, but empty—was much help. There
were facts, but so scarce and vague, and by now so
thumbed and hammered, as to be unrecognizable.
And the problem of the letter writing was undimin-
ished. But how much letter writing was there? How
long had it been going on? How many letters were
burned, thrown down the lavatory? And how many
were kept, reread, pored over? Even enjoyed? The
whole thing had been frightened underground by three-
times-repeated banging and poking by the police.

What facts there were were boring. For instance,
the letters were composed in the classic way of letters,
with words clipped from the local paper—the one he
had bought. Helpful! But nobody seemed to have
thought much about the style, though it interested him.
The language was quite practiced, that of somebody,
one would say, accustomed to putting words on paper.
Yet stiff and cramped—not a habit of personal letters.
Not an unschooled person—no spelling mistakes, and
carefully accurate punctuation—too careful; it was
painful. The letters were formal, self-conscious, gram-
matical, but with no eye for a simple everyday word.
The style of someone who thinks that a television
announcer is the perfect model.

There was no real obscenity, either, in the verbal sense. A dirty-minded bourgeois. The majority of the letters that had been found were to women, but some were to men. Hm, youngish married women. Were they simply quicker to bring such things to light? Apart from the three "victims," there was little known about these women. They were not suspected of anything.

This chasing after suspects was always a bore. He was always more interested in victims.

A fat lot of good it had done here looking for suspects. That part of the inquiry had been to his mind most thoroughly botched up. They had found one really juicy, promising suspect, and had ended up with a fist full of gravel. They'd gone on the classical supposition that someone who writes sexy letters to women is likeliest to be an elderly bachelor. When they found, on the doorstep, an elderly bachelor, with eccentric habits, a peculiar past, and a secretive nature, they stuck to him with a stupid obstinacy. Well, he was certainly interesting.

The idea of a woman writer had never been taken seriously. Yes, perhaps poison-pen letters are traditionally an elderly spinster's work, but all the elderly spinsters around seemed irreproachable. And though there was jealousy in the letters it was directed at the men, not at the women. A Lesbian in Drente? Pooh, pooh.

There had been a hunt for psychopaths, of course, and anyone who had ever been caught in a moral scandal, however slight. The State Recherche—very, very thorough indeed—had even unearthed the fact that the burgomaster, earlier in his career, had once been thought rather too fond of sitting little girls on his lap. Charming: Burgomaster Humbert N. Petit of Larousse, Illinois. But nothing had ever been seriously proved, and there was certainly no evidence, not a scrap, to link him with any of this.

After Motive, they had, with relish, attacked Opportunity. They had reached vast numbers of conclusions, and proved nothing whatever one way or the other.

Van der Valk let out a sort of moan. This might be intensely funny, but he wasn't at all sure he was greatly amused.

Arlette was busily packing her precious phonograph records.

6

The first working days, in Zwinderen, were spent observing the manners and customs of Drente, Van der Valk feeling like an anthropologist among the Papuans. Ethnological studies, indeed. He felt a bit like the schoolboy who wrote on his examination paper, "Customs beastly . . . manners none," and left it at that.

But he had a suitcase filled with books, newspaper clippings, and perfectly genuine files from the Ministry of the Interior, which he was agreeably surprised to find passionately interesting.

What, in Zwinderen, did they buy, wear, eat, drink, approve of? It wasn't, right from the start, at all what Arlette bought, wore, ate, drank, or approved of. For information about all sorts of eccentric things, often simply because he had noticed something and been puzzled, he went to the burgomaster's secretary; she was the greatest help. She knew everybody and everything, seemed never to be at a loss, and was quite willing to instruct a responsible functionary. Perhaps it flattered her sense of importance, which was needless; she was important. Of course, as confidential secretary she had access to all but the most important decisions, and that meant virtually everything that concerned the little town. She knew, too, all the local politics.

From her he learned of the long-standing quarrel between the Head of Parks and Gardens and the Municipal Gasworks. She knew the whole history of the throat-cutting between the contractors for the new garden suburb, and the figures of the loss taken by the subcontractor in electrical equipment for the sake of Prestige; it had been she who had seen that he had tried to make up the loss by skimping the workmanship. She was illuminating about the solitary Communist member of the council, about the row over the new hospital equipment, which all the doctors claimed was inadequate, about too much having been spent on the swimming bath, and got back by economizing on the new garbage trucks. She seemed to wave a scepter over everybody. The burgomaster swore by her tact and ability. Miss Burger could always get it done.

Arlette was tedious, bombarding everything with sarcasms. The Mimosastraat, to begin with.

"Why Mimosa? And why is there a mimosa street in every piddling town in Holland? None of these people have ever seen mimosa in their lives. Dahlias, tulips, narcissi I'd find understandable."

Dear Arlette. She came from the *départment* of

the Var and thought that all the mimosa in the world was her own personal property.

Curses were heaped upon the anthracite stove, though it was modern; upon the curtains in the bedroom, which did, it was true, have an aggressively rural flower pattern; upon the "three-piece suite," a bargain, soiled after being used for a model house by a local emporium; upon the extraordinary shower in the bathroom. He admitted her right about that; one was supposed to sit, apparently, in a kind of pit at waist level —a masterpiece of plumbing that would rouse an incredulous guffaw even at the sources of the Amazon.

By the third day, she was settling, moving furniture with zest, as though determined to leave, even here, her individual stamp on this borrowed anonymous shoe box of a house. But she was still acid at meals.

"Milk here's undrinkable." Aha, it was one of his items of knowledge, which he had brought out of his rag bag of Drents lore.

"Seems they like it like that. Call it 'High-pasteurized.'"

"Which to me means scorched. Butter—rendered cowhide. And the butchers! People live here, I think, on fat salt pork and mince." "Mince" is nearly the dirtiest word in Arlette's vocabulary.

"But what I find worst of all is the way they stare. Stare, stare, blatantly, openly, uncaring. Stand there transfixed with great dull eyes, gaping."

It was true. Even at Van der Valk, who was, one would say, a harmless-looking object. Here an Amsterdamer, it seemed, was an Indian from the Peruvian uplands, plus blanket and llama. The peasants did stare consumedly; little girls poked at each other and dissolved in giggles. Poor Arlette, with her accent that became strong in shops, and she still said "in a box" when she meant canned. And her hair in a fringe, with a beret on top. The women here wore scarves over hair like a dust mop, and the "ladies" wore wonderful hairy hats. They asked for a pound of mince, and obediently took what they were given. Van der Valk felt a little sorry for the butcher. Arlette's butcher had for years been accustomed to her poking, coming behind the counter, even pursuing him into his own cold room. He was used by now to "Too fresh again," and kept her steak a week longer than anyone else's.

"Be discreet," Van der Valk told her. "Be disguised." Still, he trundled about all day in a gray suit, clutching a briefcase of crude imitation pigskin, and even he was stared at. "They look," he said, "and guess immediately that your name is neither Unk nor Flook and that you don't belong to the clan."

"I am discreet. I burst myself with it. I found Beaujolais, so called, but in Albert Heijn, so it might well be drinkable. Dear Albert, his shop is to me a home from home."

Leek soup for supper, and chicory salad—not a very Drents meal, despite the presence of undoubtedly Drents butter. He settled down for a good go at the letters. Arlette had been much reconciled by discovering that one could get German television here; he had hired a set for her that morning, and she was busy with the new toy. The letters were very boring. He found himself staring entranced at the delightful hair styles of the German announcer-girls. But we must be resolute.

The longest file was the first suicide. She had been
the wife, poor girl, of the technical director—second
in command—of the little electronics factory; the
man who, with the owner, made up the inventive
team. What did they know about him? Reinders, Will;
forty-three. Came from Dordrecht. Impressive engi-
neering qualifications; evidently a brilliant chap.
Religion, Reformed. Well-regarded in his profession.
Locally spoken of as calm and steady. Mixes very little
with Zwinderen notables, but said to be friendly and
easy to get on with. Very dedicated, takes profession
very seriously; certainly a coming man. Alone or
with the boss (who lives in Baarn, but comes up at least
twice a week), makes frequent trips all over Holland and abroad. Point is that wife was often alone.
Absolutely no police record—what a blameless individual.

Wife's name Betty; thirty-six; born in Groningen;
religion, Reformed; first marriage. No children.
Churchgoer, whereas husband was not, but thought of
as a little flighty, even frivolous. Active, however, in
various do-good social activities. There had been a
rumor that she had got too friendly with a young
draftsman at the factory, who had as a consequence
been sacked. But this had not been taken very seriously, since the letters did not threaten her with any
such thing as a scandal. It was the husband who was
threatened. He was, according to the writer, a dirty
dog, and the implication was that the writer would
make the girl a much more satisfactory lover. Mm.

The letters had been found in her jewelry box after
her death—not the first to come to light, but the first
series. Was it a series? There was no way of telling.

Undated, and no way of fixing even a chronological order. There had, moreover, been phone calls, and after the first contact there were few letters—if they were, indeed, all here.

Naturally, every possible indication had been followed up. Nothing for him there. Just that hint in the style that appeared to have struck nobody much.

"You may be of opinion . . . I am well aware with what he is occupied . . . your position of standing . . . wallow in corruption and hypocrisy . . . was that not an agreeable surprise?" A sort of old-fashioned commercialese. All the letters had the same tone—a kind of affectionate menace. Offers of "rescue" and "protection." Frequent references to the "Eye of God" and the "Ear of God"—both, apparently, the writer. The later letters were lyrical about the joys of being in bed together, but nothing showed definitely whether these joys were anticipatory or reminiscent.

The police had raced to the director of the lunatic asylum for a psychiatric opinion. He had read the letters, shrugged, and said, reasonably, that the writer might well be insane but he had no opinion to offer on the basis of these letters alone. Handwriting would have given more and sharper indications, but "I have no judgments beyond those of any normal detached person, without more to go on."

Quite. The letters were mildly crazy, in much the same way as the letters of a fanatic about racing pigeons or model airplanes. It was no more and no less, to his mind, than the frustrated gentlemen who make indecent propositions to telephone-service girls. Even the explicit remarks could be total fantasy.

One letter had a different tone. It was in the dos-

sier but there was no proof that the writer was the
same. It might have been someone who had had a letter and decided to take a leaf out of the book. It was
to a young girl of sixteen; there had been an earlier
letter which she had destroyed, terrified. Recon-
structed, it read, more or less:

"You little fool. I saw you. Unless you do what I
tell you, everything will be known. Show this to no
one, but watch carefully for the next, and do exactly
what I tell you."

The one in the dossier read, "Cross the bridge tonight at nine exactly. You will get instructions at the
right moment. Wear your beige coat, but under it,
you are not to wear any clothes at all." It had gone too
far. Shocked even more than frightened, the girl had
done nothing, but had finally gone to her mother, who
had the sense to go straight to the police. Too late,
and there had been no more letters. It was one of the
first that had come to light, and had remained dis-
connected.

That looked simply like the work of some elderly
voyeur. Possibly.

There was only one other series anything like complete. The unfortunate woman who had gone out of
her mind. She sat all day in apathy; there was nothing to be got out of her. She had been the wife of a
Protestant minister, and quite a mild, reasonable
one at that; not one of the hell-fire sects. A man
against whom there had never been a breath of scandal. This was a puzzle. The letters were all full of religion. But if, say, Reinders was attacked for being an
enemy to religion—which often seemed the tone—
why attack a man known to all as deeply devout? The

unhappy man had renounced his living and vanished into obscurity. Police had questioned him, but had nothing to hold him for. He had upheld vehemently that there was no truth in any of the suggestions.

He was one of the few men to have had letters: "Do you think that nobody knows about the book of photographs in the locked bookcase? Your wife would be interested. Perhaps I will tell everybody. You would get an enthusiastic reception on Sunday then." He had not told the wife. He had done nothing. He had not understood why his wife should have acted strangely. He had disregarded the letter as a ridiculous untruth from someone evidently insane.

Why keep it?

To show the police in case there were more.

Had it never occurred to him that his wife might also have had letters?

No, it hadn't, unhappily.

Had he been afraid to draw attention to the suggestion? Was it true?

The wife's letters were much the same as Betty's: "If you do not want the scandal to ring through the whole country, you must follow the instructions you will receive implicitly."

Had she? Had anything happened? Was it all just wish fulfillment?

The other suicide—wife of the manager of the milk-products business—had left no letters. It was only an assumption that she had had any.

Van der Valk thought she had. The husband had acted rather queerly, to his mind.

Police actions had been based on mutual acquaintance. What persons had been in contact with all these

others? Remarkably many, but none of them remotely
suggestive. Whose telephone to tap, whose house to
watch? Every idea had petered out.

The whole affair had been kept from the public
—but a lot was certainly known. And the public re-
acted. That large number of respectable wives who
had got touchy with each other in public. That quite
violently heated audience in a rather scruffy café
where, on two occasions (meaning that two had been
proved), a woman had done a decidedly daring strip-
tease. Who knew what went on in a small town?
Everything was known, and nothing.

Everything could be seen. The Dutch, especially
the more provincial Dutch, do not draw their curtains even at night. There are many explanations of
this. Van der Valk had always thought it was due to
anxiety—the Dutch neurosis. The anxiety lest anyone
think them not normal, not conforming, not respectable.

"We have nothing to hide," announce those curtains.
Hadn't they? Nothing?

There is a favorite Dutch pastime that is called
"shadow watching." Everybody in Zwinderen does it,
Van der Valk had already noticed. As the name im-
plies, it is an evening occupation, toward twilight. You
sit by your own open curtains, one lamp in your room
lit, and you observe.

Every home has huge windows, front and back.
The walls are paper-thin. There is almost nothing one
can do that is not seen and heard instantly—and as
for flats . . . This could be called a typical small-town
provincial crime. And given a mildly deranged person,
of whom there are considerable numbers anywhere,

you arrived with unpleasant ease at multiple death. Which, however provincial, is as frightening, as horrid, as difficult to stop, and as worrying to authority as the classic psychopath multiple murderer of cities. Jack the Ripper, Franz Becker and all the other textbook cases. What was the difference between knifing a prostitute, strangling a child, and badgering a housewife into insanity or suicide?

People died, didn't they?

Resolutely, he shut the file, with its thick supplement of police conclusions. They were really pretty inept. He got inept conclusions, too, but he tried not to let other people read them. There is the written report that is intelligent, and there is the written report that at least sounds intelligent.

Example of ineptitude: a reference in one letter was to "eleven tomorrow." An annotation put the illuminating query "Is this a Saturday?" Meaning that if the letter writer was an employed person, Saturday would be his only free morning.

Ve-r-y helpful.

Further down, they had all gone on an assumption that since most of these people were roughly classifiable as bourgeoisie, the writer would be either self-employed or in a position to find free time at any moment of the day if he wished. Not only inept, asinine. But incidentally it had helped to thicken the blanketing haze of suspicion around the one promising suspect: a certain Mr. Besançon. He reached for the file on Mr. Besançon. Arlette, who has the un-Dutch idea that tea at night is bad for one, had made two glasses of fresh lemonade with the peel in it, and honey.

"Honey, honey?" She thinks this funny. Funny,

honey. There was a lot of very attractive steam. He fished out his lemon peel and chewed on it in a greedy way.

7

It began with an elaborate summary. Points indicating or supporting suspicion. And, to be fair of course, points in favor. Which were, briefly, that no ground existed beyond stupid prejudice to suspect the man of anything at all.

There followed a pretty complete picture of his present circumstances, and a long row of dockets—all that was known of his extraordinary checkered past. Van der Valk read the whole thing, absorbed. Very, very interesting indeed. The man was in his sixties. Lived alone. Widower.

A stranger, a Jew, an intellectual.

Known to be nervously deranged; result of wartime experiences.

Lives in house with high wall—practically the only one in Holland. You can't see what he does all day.

Works at home, in own time, in own way, at own pleasure.

Known to take long solitary walks at night. Has also been seen at six in the morning.

Is courteous, formal, but shy and distant in relations with everybody. Seems to shun human contact.

Has telephone. Does regular work for electronics firm. Has contact with husband of dead woman number 1.

Is known as inventor of mysterious apparatus and devices.

Speaks Dutch in formal, correct, but slightly stilted way.

Speaks German perfectly, French well, Russian well.

Suspected pacifist, suspected pro-Russian. Lukewarm on alliances, patriotism. Low on political consciousness.

Practices no religion. Never been known to profess any, either Jewish or any other.

Professes, on the contrary, fear of newspapers, radios, television, parties, associations, committees, organizations. (Everything in short, that makes Dutch life so agreeable.)

There were some perfectly charming annotations here, too. "Having no newspapers in the house, access to newsprint—i.e., to cut out letters—presumed limited."

Of course, the grocer does have that habit of wrapping cabbages in old newspapers. (Arlette starts reading them instead of getting on with the cabbage.)

There is a housekeeper, a middle-aged woman, who looks after Mr. Besançon out of charity and refuses a wage. She says indignantly that any connection with revolting happenings is quite unthinkable.

During protracted interviews with many most experienced police officers, Mr. Besançon showed irritation, nervous strain, and agitation in moments of fatigue. All kept within bounds, all balanced by politeness, self-control, patience, and understanding of officers' unpleasant duties. All this is explainable by his past life, which includes interrogation by the Gestapo, years in camps, and forced labor. All the policemen agreed on this.

One last thing struck Van der Valk—and hard, because it was the one thing he would have given real
weight to. An irrational feeling. It was the final annotation by the State Recherche officer:

"I have been many times struck in course of conversation with Mr. Besançon by the conviction that
he possessed some secret. This leads me to a persistent
belief that he was the author of the crimes under investigation, but the conclusive evidence, since he is
certainly a very clever man, would be hard to find.
After two days, however, of rigorous interrogation, I
am bound to state that this feeling rests upon no factual basis and must therefore be disregarded."

That, he thought, is damned funny language from
the State Recherche. The feeling he had was so strong
that he felt he had to put it in the report. But "no
factual basis," so he feels impelled to warn any reader
of said report not to give way to unsupported suspicion. (The police had, quite handsomely, apologized
for giving Besançon several thoroughly disagreeable
weeks. He had answered politely that he understood.)

The conclusion is typical. Since there is nothing
tangible, the theory must be suppressed. Quite right;
Van der Valk had got into trouble often because of
those little men who lived in his stomach and told him
things. Remember Edward G. Robinson, in that wonderful part in *Double Indemnity*? He was right. Van
der Valk had been right, too, sometimes.

Sometimes he hadn't been right.

Anyway, he was not going to get hurt feelings just
because a constipated security officer told him not to.
If he did, it would probably be because he had been
told not to.

But he was certainly going to try and get to know Mr. Besançon. Not because he suspected him of anything. He just sounded like an interesting man, and everybody else here sounded remarkably dull.

He went back to the dossier.

Born, it began, in 1901, of a South German Jewish family that had removed itself over the centuries from Prague to Munich to Breda, in Dutch Brabant. Family were watchmakers there for the last three generations.

Apprenticed in family business, and early showed remarkable aptitude. As an adult, gained a rapidly increasing reputation for making unusual timepieces, including so-called eternal clocks. Sun-, wind-, water-powered. Progressed to specialty in ingenious time-switch mechanisms.

Had a strong amateur interest in astronomy, and built telescopes as a pastime. Formed, through all this, a connection with the firm of Carl Zeiss. Went, during the thirties, frequently to Jena, where he collaborated to some extent in the early experiments on planetariums, the artificial heavens driven by clockwork mechanisms.

Was, however, in Breda at the time of Hitler's invasion of Holland, and was promptly arrested with family. He then disappeared. Was saved from extermination—suffered by entire family down to most distant connections—by obscure agency. Possibly the firm of Zeiss signaled that his special skills were worth more to the Reich then two gold teeth.

He was, in any case, forced to work on various secret weapon projects, but was never, he recalled wryly, left on any one scheme long enough to do it either

any good or any harm. He passed from mines to
rocketry and, with another of those sudden whimsical
decisions common during that epoch, was suddenly
detached from the whole thing and brought to Berlin.
Someone, he hazarded, knew that he spoke Russian
—but there were others who did, too. He wasn't complaining. During the big Russian advance of 1944, he
was used constantly by Intelligence (Schellenburg),
but was drawn more and more into the Kaltenbrunner-
Müller orbit. His work, officially, was to penetrate
Russian Intelligence reports, working on codes and
communications, but he realized later that he had
been used in the incredibly involved system of double
agents directed by Müller.

He was, in fact, being used as one of the key figures
in secret correspondence with the Russians, but was
never allowed to see enough of the complete picture
to shed any real light or give conclusive evidence.

In the final days of the Berlin siege, he was held
prisoner in the Bunker, still in almost daily contact
with Bormann, and as the Russians entered the city,
he was shot and left for dead by a member of the Bormann entourage. He was discovered by the Russians,
patched up roughly in a military hospital, held prisoner for many months—then suddenly, inexplicably,
released; a typical Russian performance.

They had come to the conclusion, presumably, after
interrogating him, that the man would never be any
good any more. He did not know enough to be a valuable counterespionage prize, and as inventor, even as
technical craftsman, he was finished. Physically, indeed, he recovered from his head wound, but not only
did he develop a nervous disease, he also had a men-

tal block. The disease was a kind of slow degeneration of the central nervous system, something similar
to that of Parkinson. He could walk upright, but he
trembled constantly and his vision was affected He
could no longer mend an alarm clock, let alone han-
dle fine machinery. And the mental block was not so
much, perhaps, the loss of inventive capacity as of the
will to do anything, to see what made something tick.
He had holes in his memory, a kind of disassociation.
He looked at simple mechanical contrivances and
could not even remember their name or function.

He had spent, inevitably, years more in observation clinics, resettlement camps, an atom of flotsam
like many more, difficult to help, wearisome, and un-
cooperative—a nuisance, a worry, a responsibility.
He was no use to anybody any more. He had the ar-
rogance and obstinacy of the outcast. He refused to
give evidence against war criminals. What was the
use? he said. Would God not know the sheep from the
goats? Would hanging all the Germans take away
Treblinka or Babiy Yar? And what could he tell them
that they did not know by now? He would have nothing to do with other Jews. He said he wished he had
been exterminated, too—what was left of life? No
family, no job, no skill, no friends, no nothing.

In the end, he had drifted back to Holland. Not to
Breda, but wandering about vaguely, a burden on
charitable organizations that were sorry for him but
glad to get rid of him. Finally he turned up in Drente.
He liked it here, he said; there were no Jews or Chris-
tains either (a remark received charitably, like many
more).

In Zwinderen it had been the burgomaster, new

then but already energetic, who had solved the impasse,
with patience and intelligence. He had seen that nothing was any use without some scrap of independence.
He had got a pension for the man, and a disability
grant, and a compensation from Germany. And a
roof. Besançon had been delighted by the burgomaster's offer of a little cottage that belonged to the lunatic asylum, tucked in a corner of the grounds there,
damp and primitive, used in the nineteenth century to
house some turnkey. Nobody in Holland wanted that;
he did. He liked the high stone wall, the gloomy cypresses and yews. He dug in the tiny sunless garden
with his first show of enthusiasm. Rehabilitation had
begun.

He went, a little later, to the burgomaster, offering
to do any work he was still capable of. That was tactfully refused, but the offer was passed to the first factories then being established in Drente. Here he
picked up a connection; the electronics firm could use,
they said, a Russian translator from time to time. This
spread, and now there were half a dozen firms that
sent him scientific reports for translation. He had
learned pharmaceutical and chemical symbols—or re-
learned them, along with his lost mathematics—
and he was much appreciated by his employers. Nobody, they said warmly, could translate Russian or
technical German with such lucidity. Nobody could
so seize extracts, make so clear and brief a para-
phrase, so pierce the jungle of administrative or
bureaucratic phrase, so marshal the kernel of facts in
a long involved report that might cover three years'
work of a dedicated but vague scientific person behind
the Urals somewhere.

His writing was too shaky to be usable, but the grateful electronics firm designed and built a special typewriter for him; it was the owner of the firm, too, who found him a housekeeper.

Now, he said, he was happy. He worked, he earned money. He bought books and records. He took long walks and tended his garden. Occasionally someone from "his" firms came to consult him on some point; he saw nobody else. He had been invited to people's houses; he came courteously and behaved perfectly, but let it be understood that he preferred not to come. People had learned to respect his small eccentricities.

Of course, when he appeared in the village, as he sometimes did for gum or string, carbon paper or a pair of socks, children whooped and people whispered. He was used by the peasantry as a bogeyman; many a tiny Drents cropped-head was threatened with "the Russian professor." But his manner, indifferent, formal, always courteous, conquered even peasant suspicions. When he raised his hat so politely to some dummy mottled milkmaid behind the pencils and envelopes, pointing with a shaky forefinger at a roll of sticking tape, he could hardly be thought of as bogey. He had been there ten years by now. He had got shakier, his eyesight worse. He could still walk upright, but uncertainly, with a stick. But mentally he had not failed.

He wore corduroy trousers like the workmen; cheap ready-made coats;- he had a "good suit" indistinguishable from that of the local churchwarden. He had experimented with hats, and wore at present an extraordinary green thing, Dutch Tyrolean, cut from fuzzy cardboard. He sometimes shuffled out in the wooden shoes he used for gardening.

There was nothing about him, though, of the comic-strip absent-minded scientist. His hair was cut short and he used a clothesbrush vigorously. He was, in his sixties, trim, neat, and tidy; a small thin man with authority still in his carriage. He had fine flowers behind his high gray wall, and on the sunny side a cherry tree facing the little window of his living room. The little cottage was only two rooms, with a sort of lean-to kitchen at the back and a septic-tank lavatory across a tiny yard. He had electricity but no gas.

He always wore dark glasses over his sharp blue eyes. The doctor had given him maybe another five years. These nervous degeneration diseases are deadly, but extremely slow. He hoped, he said, to have another two years of useful work.

He had been examined dozens of times by every conceivable sort of neurologist and psychiatrist. Perfectly sane, perfectly lucid. Remarkably well adjusted to severe trauma.

Might such a person write threatening obscene letters to respectable married women and creep about peering and listening for some little human misdeed or indiscretion?

Even if he might, he hadn't known any of the women, or anything about them. But a theory had been built up by some artful imbecile of a policeman. The electronics firm manufactured, among other specialized gadgets, tiny microphones and listening posts of incredible power and sensitivity. One of their recent efforts could (classified, highly secret, but the policeman had wormed out certain facts), pick up conversational tones at twenty yards or more, through the walls of houses. Even disregarding the legend that former-engineer Besançon was a conjuring-trick king, had he ever, through his work, had access to any such thing? It had been investigated; the answer was definitely negative. He had never even been in the factory. Still, it was a seductive notion. How else had the letter writer found out some of the things he appeared to know?

"Time to go to bed," said Arlette, yawning. "There's been a good variety show from Munich. My German's getting better, but that Bavarian dialect is beyond me. Come on, get unglued."

PART TWO

ACQUAINTANCE

1

HAVING READ THE EXHAUSTIVE dossier, and being quite
convinced that the man had nothing whatever to do
with writing naughty letters, it was, Van der Valk
admitted, a pure waste of time to go and see him.
Quite unjustifiable. But he was enjoying the sensation
of doing unjustifiable things; there was nobody shouting at him to justify. It was not just vulgar curiosity
that took him in Besançon's direction next day. He had
to see for himself—and was it the expectation, too, of
finding somebody human at last in this spot? He
thought that his alias would be enough to get him into
the little fortress behind the wall of the lunatic asylum. And what then? He had no idea.

It was at the point just outside the town where the
bog had been halted. Pavements petered out, street
lighting stopped abruptly, and the muddy digging of
foundations for new houses gave way to sodden
fields and sparse tormented trees, with uninviting

drainage ditches every hundred yards. A gate in the high wall had an admonishing notice about "Unauthorized Persons"; he peered.

Nothing exciting—fields. Evidence that the lunatic asylum had cows, grew vegetables, and kept chickens. A roadway led to a ragged belt of poplars, behind which he could see bits of a vast dingy building. He went on along the road, after a minute reached a corner, and sure enough around the corner he found another gate, and could see evergreens over the wall. The gate was a rusty iron affair, backed with a sort of "blindage" of galvanized metal that blocked the view between the bars. He greatly envied Mr. Besançon all this privacy. He found an old chain dangling among ivy tendrils, pulled, and heard a cowbell tinkle.

A woman in an apron, sturdy, shapeless. She wore spectacles, was apple-cheeked, had straggly brown hair—a Dutch woman like five million more. She approved of his taking his hat off and extending one of the mumbo-jumbo cards.

"He's working, but if you'll come in I'm sure he'll— Do you mind just waiting here?" Yes; the door opened straight into the living room. Van der Valk admired the flower borders, though it was February and there was little to see. Even on the shadowed, drippy side of the garden, where thick brambly undergrowth was enough to cut off the view of the asylum altogether, there were rhododendrons and azaleas.

"Will you please come in?" She bustled off toward a nice smell of stew. He bowed, said good morning, and turned to shut the door. A thin neat man, in old trousers and a baggy jacket, had got up politely. One got a fleeting first impression of short gray hair, a face with very deep sunken wrinkles but a powerful energetic mouth, and eyes that still flashed behind the dark glasses.

"Good morning." Voice deep and resonant.

"My name is Van der Valk. I'm from the Ministry of the Interior. My field of study includes town planning. There is no need to trouble you, but since I was passing . . ."

"But please sit down. Allow me to take your hat." There were two shabby armchairs with a coffee table between them and a standard lamp. Mr. Besançon sat at his desk again and examined his guest calmly. It was strange; Van der Valk at once had the feeling that he was sitting in the wrong chair. As a policeman, it was his business to sit behind desks and look at people that way. The man was immediately impressive; he had a patient watchfulness. Van der Valk launched into a gabble about possible demolition of the asylum, possible road widening; blah-blah.

"Am I scheduled for demolition?"

"That is too sweeping. In the event of such a decision, you would be notified well in advance. If you objected, you would have every opportunity to put your case." Mild smile, faintly raised eybrows.

"I am attached to this house, strangely."

"Do not disquiet yourself. No decision has yet been made or will be made for quite a time. I really only came to sound your opinion."

"My opinion is that I will not live very long. If these changes are postponed a year, I shall, I think, have very little to say. I am attacked, I must tell you, by a slow but mortal disease. But I should be happy if I were left in peace for what time I have left."

"I think I can guarantee you some years without interruption." Van der Valk sincerely hoped that no municipal busybody really did have a road-widening project; it was perfectly possible.

Again the faint smile. "More than enough . . . I suppose that you have informed yourself about my circumstances?"

"I have access to all information normally available to the Ministry," sounding correctly prim. Van der Valk thought he was doing this quite well.

"Just so."

"Such details are necessarily incomplete."

"So you make a point of calling on people who may live—let's say along a road scheduled for rebuilding."

"When we can."

"That is conscientious. And courteous. My experience of Ministry officials is that they frequently have both qualities, but that their function seems to prevent the free exercise of either." My turn for the faint smile. Really, this fellow was shrewd.

"We do our best. It is painful to be criticized for what, to the uninformed eye, simply looks like turning defenseless people out of their homes."

"Painful, but the state functionary grows an extra skin. Perhaps they have to. I am very grateful that you should spare the time to call on me."

"We learn"—Van der Valk thinking he was being sly—"to make time our servant. The wheels of Ministries are slow."

"Ah." Reflective nod. "You have plenty of time. Most functionaries bustle, always in a hurry. You have a bird's-eye view—in a manner of speaking—of peo-

ple as well as sites, streets, ciphers, statistics. Most interesting."

"Certainly." Van der Valk did not quite get the
drift but admired the way Besançon was cross-
examining him—in a manner of speaking.

"Perhaps my experience has been too one-sided. It
is the lower echelon, is it not, that adopts that bustling
air, that fiction that there is never time for anything,
that determination to obliterate the individual. The
tiny self-importance of the village postmaster; once he
has a rubber stamp in his hand, he imagines that he
embodies all the dignity of the State. Whereas you are
plainly a senior official."

"That is so." Van der Valk was being driven like a
sheep, and interested enough not to care.

"Since you are not in a hurry"—inexorably—"may
I offer you a cup of coffee?"

"That would be kind."

"I will ask Mrs. Bakhuis—she generally brings me
some.

"I am tempted to think"—coming back with deliberate steps; the trembling was noticeable, but not
disconcerting—"that as a general rule policemen, perhaps, are fortunate among state servants in having
more obligatory contact with human beings. Even
rather objectionable humans, who smell, who could do
with delousing, are preferable to none."

"And yet, if I am to believe what I hear, you are
not very fond of the human race."

"There have been times, you see, when I smelled
and needed delousing. A thing quite inconceivable
to a civil servant. The pressure upon functionaries to
spend more and more time shut away in little cells,

monastically devoted to their in and out trays—it is hardly fair on them."

Van der Valk felt like saying right out what he had come for. What was the point of fencing further? This man was not guilty of any little, nutty, pathetic crimes. But he had to play the scene out a bit.

"Aren't you tending toward special pleading? Every type of state servant has his particular problems. His questions, call it, of conscience."

He did not answer. He studied his guest with a placid look. Van der Valk studied the surroundings. There were no pictures, but there were many home-made bookshelves. Lots of books, rows of cardboard files, doubtless containing his work, a shelf full of records. Tidy, for a man who lived alone. A shabby poverty, but not genteel, not ashamed. Those books were in all the major languages of Europe, and they looked well handled.

Why were there no pictures? Did the man prefer things heard to things seen? Mrs. Thing came in with a pleasant smile and two cups of coffee. Van der Valk often wondered why the Dutch keep the coffeepot in the kitchen, as though it were something to be ashamed of.

The door behind the housekeeper shut; they stirred their coffee. Van der Valk offered him a cigarette, which he shook his head at slightly. The policeman had a feeling they were coming to the point.

"Functionaries," Van der Valk said. "Good or bad, sensitive or not. One thing they all have in common is their professionalism. In the last analysis, they're getting paid for it."

He had been expecting the reaction, but not that it would be so direct.

"Are you by any chance a policeman?"

To that kind of question, one cannot hesitate or shuffle.

"Yes."

"I have been visited by so many, you see," politely.

"That you penetrate me so easily shows that I can't be a new kind."

"The first to be frank."

"Perhaps I have started work with a different assumption. You don't fit my notions of this type of crime."

"What type of crime?"

"You mean you don't know?"

"I have never been told"—simply—"what it was that I was suspected of doing or being."

"Oh dear. I suppose that's typical. You were suspected of being the author of anonymous blackmailing letters."

Van der Valk was watching closely; a very strange expression passed rapidly over the strong facial muscles. He could not quite put a name to it. Relief from apprehension?

"How stupid I am not to have guessed, after all the questioning."

"I am surprised you didn't." Van der Valk was, too; the man was intelligent; more than that he thought.

"I am an innocent fellow; it simply never occurred to me. Now, of course, I realize that I am an obvious suspect. Eccentric, probably mentally deranged, slightly sinister to village eyes— Aha, now I see."

"Why do you call yourself sinister?"

"In a village . . . A Jew, living behind a wall, avoiding people. I had understood that I would be suspect."

"But it bothered you, to be suspect?"

"No, not really. Only peasant supersititon."

"Quite so. Yet you were worried."

"Worried at the unceasing pressure of suspicion from officials. That is not superstition. It is, also, a hard fact. Relays of policemen, always increasing in importance. The last were State Recherche. What would those gentlemen have to do with anonymous letters?"

"Two people have died—and the matter has still not been cleared up. The authorities have taken this seriously. It is vague, obscure."

"I see. And you do not suspect me of anything still?"

Van der Valk got up. "I try never to suspect anybody of anything. I try to wait until I know."

"I have grown oversensitive."

"I can see that. But will it worry you if I come back?"

"You do, then, suspect me of something."

"No. I just like talking."

"Come whenever you like. I am always here—but I am at a loss to see how that can profit you."

"Everything profits me. And I like unusual people. They force one to think about things." Van der Valk picked up his hat. He could see well enough that Besançon preferred to be left alone, but he knew that he would not show him hostility now that he knew who he was. Using this man as a sparring partner would lighten his days, here in Zwinderen. Too bad if the man didn't like it.

2

The Mimosastraat, where Van der Valk now lived, was a street exactly like ten thousand other streets in Holland, and probably identical to a thousand other mimosa streets. Tiny two-storied houses in two neat bricky rows, patterned into little parcels of six at a time. One saw through the huge windows to a further street, and through that again to infinity. Exactly like the Droste cocoa tin. Painted on it is a nurse holding another cocoa tin, with a nurse on it ...

Miniature balconies wih iron railings, over the front door; miniature gardens with a few bulbs and a strip of grass. A grass border between path and road. When Van der Valk got home, there were already four Volkswagens standing neatly parked in the road. All the houses were identical; he wondered which was his. The Mimosastraat is Holland.

He stopped and studied the street: Van der Valk's brooding, piercing aquiline look; Michelangelo contemplating the Saint Peter. He looked, much more likely, as though struck with amnesia, paralysis of the motor nerves, or perhaps just as though he had a crick in his back.

A child's scooter had been flung down on the grass; two families had not yet taken in their trash cans. A little girl had tied a string to a fence, and was holding the free end very solemnly and seriously, watching another little girl jumping over it in a complicated, important procession of steps. A bigger girl, in tartan

trousers she had grown out of, was roller skating with
the sudden ducking lurch and widespread fingers of
the beginner, watched with admiration by two tiny
ones in woolly tights. Very pink cheeks and naughty
eyes peeping out of the hoods of their windbreakers;
moisture forming on curls in front; bright Norwegian
mittens. One of them was rather bowlegged.

Others could gaze, too; he felt the pressure of
twenty pairs of unseen eyes prickling over the skin on
the back of his neck. He locked the car door, picked
up the good briefcase, and scampered for his door—
crinkle glass badly set in flimsy softwood painted a
depressing yellow.

The muslin curtains of the house across the street
flickered as he turned to shut the door. Those eyes
were able to count the stitches that were darned into
his left sock last week.

There was a good smell of *pot-au-feu;* celery,
leeks, turnips, onions puttering gently. Arlette was
gazing fascinated at German children's television; the
film had been dubbed, with the charming result of an
English bobby, pot hat and all, out in the midday sun
but talking forthright Kölner German. Arlette had
bought a plant, a feathery little cocos palm that flut-
tered in the draft, and he shut the door hastily.

"I've been writing to the boys, telling them all the
frightful things that are happening to us. And I
bought some smoked eel. We're going to have a nice
evening—*Così Fan Tutte,* from the new theatre in
Frankfort."

Which pleased him very much. He wasn't in a
thinking mood. Tomorrow, anyway, was only a boring

trek around pastures a lot of oxen had nibbled pretty bare.

3

The next morning was bright and sunny. Even when the wind is from the west, it is often sunny in Holland. It is a false promise, for already before midday a gray pall of cloud will have blanketed the sky, a cold little wind will be searching one's bones at street corners, stirring up dust, and presently rain will turn the dust to mud again. But while it lasts, the sunshine cheers everybody. It has the thin, bright texture of morning, and accompanies a whole happy orchestra of morning noises. The loud crash of trash cans being emptied into the creeping garbage truck, a strange animal that digests suburban refuse by standing on its head and then yawns toothily for more. The clattering three-wheeler of the milkman, seeming far too burdened for its very tiny, incredibly noisy motor. The milkman sits upon this poor beast wearing an extraordinary sort of Australian bush hat against the elements, and scribbles busily in his little book as he bumps over the uneven brick; it's a total mystery how the writing can be legible even to him. Presently he will jump off, bang lustily on a bell that came off the Inchape Rock, and pretend to be a Caribbean steel band, exactly as though he had come creeping on slippers and wanted to give the housewives a start.

Building sites give whoops on their hooters, telling workmen who are already, probably, stretched out playing cards (strange how workmen seem the same all over the world), that they can have a coffee break.

There is an uproar from school playgrounds, where the children (also the same everywhere) shriek in a thin, piercing tone that is as well very much a morning noise.

Driving the Volkswagen down the falsely genial shopping street, Van der Valk felt like a Mexican on his donkey. Housewives riding bikes, pushing bikes, lugging tiny children off the backs of bikes—all in the middle of the road and paying not the least attention either to him in his tiny black-beetle auto or to Albert Heijn's truck, which is ten feet tall and thirty feet long. The housewives are busy with the shopping. They stand in the middle of the road staring at the bargains of the day, announced on bits of cardboard propped against a condensed-milk pyramid; loud, red-colored, and misspelled. There are unheard-of, un-repeatable, unique opportunities to get two pieces of soap and a toothbrush free if one just buys two of the new giant-size boxes.

Are housewives, he wondered, even more naïve than usual when the sun shines? There was a broad-beamed soul sticking well out into the road, a globu-lar toddler with its eyes popping out clutched in her muscular armpit, forcing a cabbage into her bicycle basket. She glared, rather as though it were his fault that she couldn't get it in. Perhaps she would now try clutching the cabbage and stuffing the toddler.

This was Drente, too, but Van der Valk didn't think it was the real Drente. It looked identical to everywhere else in Holland, and could just as easily have been the Jan Galenstraat in Amsterdam West. There were housewives with anonymous pieces of meat, neatly squeezed into a plastic pillowcase that

makes any ragged old strip of draft ox look succulent
and as though it deserved to be so expensive, and a
quarter-pound of liver sausage and a quarter-pound
of soapy cheese, both cut very thin on the bacon
slicer, and a packet of smelly biscuits for this afternoon with the tea.

He got stuck behind another vast truck, containing,
to judge from the huge curly letters written on it,
nothing but several million JELLYBABIES. But at last
he was at the top of the street. He disregarded the one
tree-shaded road in Zwinderen, where the houses
of the managerial class are—interesting though this
was—and went on past the railway station and the
milk factory next door. Here a road, broad and bare,
brand-new, had been driven into the soggy countryside. It had no pavements, but there was a wide
bricked bicycle path on each side. This was the "industry terrain." No houses here, but neat factories on
both sides, prim, quiet, and abandoned-looking. More
trucks here, standing like oxen with their trailers behind them. A goods truck on a spur line standing by a
loading platform, and two overalled characters lan-
guidly stacking cardboard crates. Through the fields
behind ran the canal, and a faint noise reached Van
der Valk from where a suction line was unloading
sand and gravel barges for the Readymixed Konkrete
Company.

He reached the electronics factory and parked the
auto where it said "Executives Only," outside a towering wall of glass window through which nothing
could be seen at all. There was a strong smell of packing materials from a loading bay; corrugated cardboard and gummed sealing strip and stenciling ink. A

notice told him "STATE YOUR BUSINESS AT THE TIME-
KEEPER'S OFFICE," which adjoined a shed full of non-
executive bikes.

Three minutes later he was being ushered into the
owner-director's office. This was not as lucky as it
sounds; he had found out from Miss Burger that he
had regular days.

"What can I do for you, Mr. Uh? From The Hague,
I see. Ethnographic survey, huh?" Brightly and a little
cunningly, as though he knew all about those surveys.

"Yes. We are naturally anxious to follow all the—
er, trends that may be stimulated by setting up industry here. Housing, transport, leisure activities of work-
ers—er, retail outlets." Splendid phrase; Van der Valk
was not quite sure what it meant.

"Quite, quite. And how can I help you? You want
to interview the personnel or something?" Van der
Valk leaned forward with a sharp disapproving nose.

"This conversation is confidential and inviolable."
The owner looked startled, as Van der Valk had intended. He was one of these knowing businessmen
with a hoarse chuckling voice.

"Certainly, if you wish. We're quite undisturbed
here." Van der Valk passed one of his real cards
across the desk and enjoyed the reaction.

"Inspector . . . Central Recherche . . . What's this
about? I've made no complaint. We've had no troubles. As far as I know, we've broken no laws."

"Glad to hear it, but I'm interested neither in pecu-
lation nor the maximum agreed wage. I'm interested
in the death of your technical director's wife."

"Oh, my God. You mean this ethnographic survey
is—"

"In this town I am an official of the Ministry of the Interior. I mean to stay that way. There've been more than enough policemen already."

"How I agree. Poor Betty. But I fail to see—"

"You aren't under any suspicion. This is verbal, informal, confidential, just like my own identity. Whatever you may say is not stenographed."

"But I've told the police anything I knew—precious little, incidentally."

Van der Valk believed in pushing this kind of person off balance when possible. "I should like you to tell me the things you've suppressed in previous meetings with the police," pleasantly.

"I've suppressed nothing, damn it."

"Generally called forgetting—often truly, at that. I'm not calling you a liar, but this affair concerns the life of everyone in this town."

"But not mine, man."

"Everyone."

"Damn it, I don't even live here. I come here two days, maybe three, a week. Reinders lives here. He's the man you want."

"But I chose to start with you. You stay the night here sometimes?"

"Well, yes, occasionally, when Will and I were working on a problem."

"And where, then? Not in a hotel?"

"Well, no; they're ghastly."

"At Will's house, then? Normal, natural, understandable—and much more comfortable."

"I'm not trying to conceal it," defensively.

"You called her Betty, equally naturally."

"You've no objection, I hope."

"Quite the contrary, I'm delighted. Ever sleep with her?"

That got to him. A businessman, flabbergasted.

"Don't give yourself the trouble of looking shocked."

He hoisted the expression off the floor and wrestled with it a moment.

A small smile crept out. "Well . . . I was just thinking that the last set of policemen circled around that very question without quite daring to ask it, and you come plumb straight out. The answer is no. And what's more she was a very conscientious woman, and I don't believe her boy friend did either."

"Why exactly did you fire him, since as I understand there was no great gossip or scandal caused?"

"In the first place, because he wasn't a particularly good craftsman. Second, because Will didn't."

"Will, I take it, thought it wouldn't be fair."

"Put it this way. Will wasn't going to stand for the fellow hanging about Betty, but to fire him— It might be said he had acted out of personal motives, even spite. Whereas coming from me . . . I simply told the chap he wasn't doing work of a quality that justified my paying him that much. Betty, poor innocent, thought Will knew nothing about it."

"What amuses me is that neither you nor Will are above pinching a handy bottom on a trip, but at the mildest indiscretion of the wife you're all remarkably drastic."

"We're extremely careful to cause no trouble or gossip anywhere near our homes," curtly.

Van der Valk had got the background he wanted. The two husbands, gifted, energetic, often abroad and accustomed to a circle of others equally active, had "played the part." Whiskey and call girls in the hotel suites of Düsseldorf or Milan. Half the fun was in kicking over the respectability to which they were constrained at home. The girls had meant no more than a stolen apple. Betty, a straitly reared small-town girl, had had intoxicating tastes of the men's conversation and jokes. She had got over her initial prudery and tried to play the part as well. Stuck at home, a bit neglected by a husband giving too much time to his career, having no children, she had done a few innocent, mildly silly things, but had had the bad luck to be spied out by a blackmailer who had enormously magnified it all. The tangle had grown involved; she had dreaded causing a scandal, had dreaded compromising her husband's position, and had not been able to ride out the squall. Neither the experience of life nor the firmness of character. Who knows, she had perhaps given in to the blackmailer's demands. Finally, she had seen nothing for it but sleeping pills.

"That was how it happened—you agree?"

"Yes, I rather think so, seen like that. But if only she'd told Will—or me—we'd have backed her up, of course."

Prodding this character off balance had been a success. Van der Valk decided to try a second barrel and a riskier shot.

"One more small point. Your firm produces sensitive listening gadgets for various purposes. There's a lot of mention in the police reports of one that might have been useful in a blackmailer's hands. The thing that—what does it do?"

"Listens to machinery—jet engines, to take an ex-

ample—under test. It can detect faint flutters with a
high level of exterior noise. I know what you're head-
ing at. It's nonsense."

"You maintained that no such apparatus could get
into the wrong hands."

"I did and I do."

"You don't have to tell me lies, you know. Don't
interrupt. You, and Will, occasionally take things
home. Prototypes, or whatever you call them. You
play with them at home, and you may think up a
modification or experiment on an improvement.
Right?"

"Well, that's so, within limits, but—"

"Now, it occurred to you—just as it occurred to
me; I wasn't born yesterday either—that it might be
very comic to try one of these things out in a hotel,
say? You did, and found it a good joke, and, being
a big broad-minded businessman, you had a good
laugh about this in Betty's presence. Am I wrong?"

"Completely."

"Nonsense," in an unimpressed way. "You left a
gadget—I don't say this one, but some similar bit of
apparatus—lying about in Will's house. When it disappeared, you didn't even notice at first. When you
did, you were alarmed because the thing is classified
as secret. After Betty's death you were really scared,
because it occurred to you that this thing might in
some way be connected. And you stuck to a lie
through thick and thin.

"This is all logical, natural, consequential. But
you've just denied it with such false bravado, and you
are looking so particularly guilty, that I now know that
this—ach, not necessarily in detail—is so."

"But, my God, how do you know?"

"I guessed. Look, the writer of these letters boasts of being the 'Ear of God.' That is a figurative remark; the fact is, however, that this person knows a remarkable number of things that an ordinary person would not know. The conclusion is that he got something of this sort, and presumably from or through Betty. I'm not accusing you. Now, tell me about the thing— what it looks like, how it's used."

"It's in a cigar box," much squashed, even shaken. "We chose that to act as a model for the size of the unit we wanted. We've managed to reduce the size since, but in essentials it's unchanged. It's like a transistor set—with special valves, of course. It has two loop aerials that act as direction finders, give a cross bearing, and can pinpoint a sound. It's powered by ordinary transistor batteries. It has earphones with baffles that shut out exterior sound. They weren't perfected, but at night, or anywhere with no more than an ordinary volume of sound . . . You only have to focus it on a wall or something, and choose the right distance and angle. If you get too close, you might get overriding sounds on the same bearing— I mean from farther off the angle's more acute and the bearing more precise. At about thirty feet you'd get a conversation like ours."

"So you were badly scared."

"We thought it might get used for espionage or something. Anybody could learn to use it with a little practice. Of course, it's classified; we have a model for commercial use that works at much closer quarters only, which can be built into inspection units. The Ministry would kick up a great stink. . . . When

Betty died, and then they found those letters, we—
Some policeman got the idea but we were able to deny
it."

"We'll get it back; it's not being used for espionage. But just as long as we understand each other. I
can twist your arm. You say nothing, you hear?
About this, or about me. And not even to Will. You
breathe and I'll break your neck with this."

Van der Valk stopped on the way out and gave him
his lecherous grin.

4

The sun had vanished as he came out, and there was
a raw northwesterly wind. He had still another call to
make: the manager of the milk co-operative. The
manager's office was not private, but the house ad-
joining was his home and Van der Valk decided to
work on him there. He was quite a classic type for
stiffness and conformity. Van der Valk certainly did
not suspect him of anything, but there were one or
two things in the reports he had thought a little odd,
and he had wondered whether he could use them to
lever any interesting information out of the man.

He had to wait five minutes; the manager had, it appeared, "some instructions he had to give." The
kitchenmaid put Van der Valk in the good front room,
and there he amused himself while waiting, hunting
for an elusive phrase in his mind. He caught the reference suddenly. Ernest Hemingway, an overrated
writer, but he wrote one good book at least, and
created some unforgettable characters. This man was
like one of them. Hemingway, of course, had been

talking about a Spaniard. What were the exact
words? "Heavier than mercury; fuller of boredom than
a steer drawing a cart on a country road." Fernando,
in *Bell*—peculiarly apt for this personage.

You saw it in looking around the room. It was classic, too—the provincial "good front room" of the Holland of forty years ago. Where no one ever came, bar
the dominie twice a year, and the relations for the wedding anniversary, and the daughters for their piano
practicing. Sad rooms, hatefully clean, revoltingly arranged and undisturbed, full of unseen shutters, reek-
ing of must and fust. Not one single tiny object that
was either beautiful or useful; not a scrap of fringe or
varnish that was necessary. No spontaneous, unpre-
tentious breath had ever been drawn here.

Why had the woman who had lived in this house
put her head in the gas oven? Looking at this room,
Van der Valk could hardly believe that she had made
even the trivial slip that put her in the hands of a
blackmailer. Something, he thought, had threatened
her "standing," her position of ease and assurance
among the other wives on the good-works committee
—the most precious thing in her life. But something
had so undermined that solid prop that she had lost
her footing and gone under. Provincial Holland.

The steer came into the room, fidgeted, and sat at
last uneasily on a plush chair. This was the only
room where one could be sure that the kitchenmaid
would not be able to listen.

They had given out that the wife had had an in-
curable disease. He had been much sympathized with,
the good man. Perhaps he would marry again, as soon
as standing and provincial morality approved.

Van der Valk slowly took out one of his real
cards. "I am here on the instructions of the Procureur-
Général. This whole business must be cleared up."

"It has nothing whatever to do with me."

"Your wife, alas, died."

"Whatever it is that you are investigating, uh—Inspector, I would prefer you to stop these attempts to
drag my wife's memory into disrepute."

"Ah. I quite understand. You would prefer it if
nothing more was ever said or done. Unfortunately,
I'm going through with this, regardless of whatever
must be disturbed or uncovered."

Good heaven, how the fellow sat, incrusted in virtue. Van der Valk really wanted to tell him he deserved pelting with stale eggs for producing such
lousy milk. Look at him—rancid as his own butter.

Now, that won't do, Van der Valk thought. I may
not allow these things to affect me. My feelings about
butter are not relevant to the death of a poor wretch's
unhappy wife.

"I'll do everything I can to spare you pain or publicity. You see that I have come anonymously, and
very likely I'll never worry you again. But this is
like a creeping infection—we really must cut deep.
These frightened little prods at the surface only make
things worse."

It seemed to have no effect. The fellow sat there
like a bump on a log, correct, humorless, righteous.
Van der Valk felt as though he were wading through
taffy, and plowed heavily.

"This is a judicial inquiry; you are legally required
to answer my questions. Now—correct me if these details are wrong, which I quote from official police

reports. When you found your wife, you immediately locked the whole house, you went in person to the police, and you asked for the inspector in person. You refused to speak to the uniformed agent. You did not telephone. You appeared at the bureau at eight-ten in the morning; you waited twenty minutes for the inspector and you insisted that he come alone."

"That is correct."

"Why did you not call a doctor?"

"I knew that it would serve no purpose. My wife had been exposed too long to the poisonous effects of gas. I opened the windows; I locked the doors, not only because the cleaning woman was due to arrive and might have been exposed to danger, but because it was no affair of hers."

"How did you know how long your wife had been exposed?"

"She had been in bed. I heard her go downstairs. I told the inspector that."

He had; it was in the report. She had gone down at night in her pajamas, when the husband was awake, or at least had wakened.

Had she hoped that he would find her, stop her? Van der Valk felt that he didn't know—that she had perhaps chosen this as a way of telling him. But he had fallen asleep without waiting for her to return.

A poignant aspect to the whole thing was that not only is a gas-oven death a rarity in Holland; the gas oven itself is a rarity. The Dutch seldom use ovens in their cooking. This was another example of provincial pretentiousness—an imposing gas stove, whose oven had never once been used.

Why, then, had she used it now—for the first, the

only, time? How had she heard that this is a suicide method? In England, now, it is common—and reported in the press, but she would not have known that. Had she really put her own head in the oven? Or had she been put? The State Recherche had considered this, too, but as with the other questionable points, no clear conclusion could be reached.

The man was still sitting unmoved.

"Tell me—why go to see the inspector? Why not ring your doctor and let him see to the formalities? He could have made the statutory notification to the police."

"As everybody found quite natural, Inspector. I was upset. I suppose I thought that in a case of suicide . . ."

"Is your doctor not a friend of yours?"

"Certainly he is."

"Is he no good?"

"I have complete confidence in him."

"I rather thought you had. He suggested—or, at least, concurred in—this invention of a disease. Whereas there was no disease. We know—and you know—that your wife was perfectly healthy. Therefore, I think, you went to the inspector, saying 'Come quick.' Yet you claim that you knew nothing about the letters some people have received, or that there had been another suicide—fairly recently, at that—under circumstances that were somewhat mysterious, too, or so the village gossip ran."

"I know nothing about letters, and I do not listen to gossip. I have since been told that certain persons appear to have received anonymous letters, but it has never been proved that my wife was among them. And you have no right to insinuate that she was."

"Have you had any letters?"

"No. As I have told the other officers. And I fail to see what purpose this repetition will serve."

"You can just leave me to be the judge of that. I am in authority here." It squashed him. These people are scared sick of their government.

"Well, I intended no discourtesy."

"You still maintain that it was normal to leave your wife lying on the kitchen floor while you ran for the inspector—even waiting twenty minutes for him, refusing to give details to the staff on duty?"

Not even this reached a target. He just sat, prissily.

"The inspector is an acquaintance; it seemed to me natural that my contact should be with someone I knew to be reliable."

"Reliable not to gossip?" Hell, what could he do to penetrate? Van der Valk knew it wasn't right; it didn't sound right. This fellow knew about the letters—he was damn sure of it. But how to make him talk?

Well, with the other, the engineer, a thrust had disarmed, laid open. But that was at least a highly intelligent man, and not a provincial. This man was low on intelligence. Van der Valk decided to take the stick and make a crude smash through all the careful defenses and hedges of propriety.

"Just tell me one thing."

"If I can, naturally," very stiff.

"Have you ever done anything that would give a person—any person—the smallest opening to make an accusation, to your wife or yourself? An accusation of immorality?"

He looked as though he had been slapped with a
smelly wet floor mop. "Most certainly and decidedly
not."

"Never?" Sweetly. Van der Valk picked rough, direct phrases; street words. "These nice bits you have
here in the white overalls—never kissed one of them?
Never craftily sort of slid your hand up a skirt when
no one was looking? Or that kitchenmaid—fresh,
young, nice white teeth. Quite appetizing in that tight
skirt. You could quickly slip the pants off that behind
the kitchen door; nobody would know."

Outrage, looking like a dying cod.

"How dare you—how can you— I would never
dream—I swear to you—never, never, never— Such
filth—obscenity from the mouth of an official—it's
unthinkable."

It had worked. That was truth at least.

"But the letters accused you of these things," Van
der Valk said cheerfully. The poor wretch stopped
dead.

"But I destroyed all the letters."

"Now we're getting somewhere."

"Oh . . ."

Van der Valk thought himself a dirty stinker to play
such an old low trick on a sanctified cheesemonger.

He drilled in for half an hour, and was ready to bet
at the end that the man was telling the truth. He had
not dreamed— Well, he might have dreamed, but had
certainly not dared. Not only had the wife's sharp
eyes been on godliness (next to cleanliness), but a
hundred other vinegary hawkeyes were. "Avoid the
very appearance of evil"—Van der Valk could hear
the dominie saying it mellifluously. The same one,

ironically, who had been accused of having naughty photos.

Yet even here these things were done, even in the smallest, primmest places. They had been done at Staphorst. And last year, in just such another enclosed, schismatic dorp, the accusation Van der Valk had just made had been made, too, and against a minister. By another minister.

The court had decided it was not true, and minister number 1 had caught a sharp rap for defamation. But it didn't matter whether it was true or not. Such accusations had only to be made and they were already effective. There would certainly be elderly saints ready to believe all this and more.

Just so here. These accusations were likely, even probably, not true at all. But the blackmailer had known they would be most efficacious. Whoever it was, it was someone who thoroughly understood the workings of villages.

This chap, Van der Valk felt sufficiently sure, was telling the truth and had not strayed. And wasn't that just what caught him, as it had caught his wife?

The sheer enormity of being accused of straying had paralyzed them. They had known that the very appearance of evil would ruin them.

5

Van der Valk went to see the burgomaster that evening for the first time since coming to Zwinderen. At his home, in the evening, by arrangement. The policeman left the Volkswagen a street away, deliberately, and walked to the burgomaster's house, almost a

villa, on the Koninginneweg. Queen Street. There is a
Koninginneweg in every town in Holland, just like the
Mimosastraat. It is grander, that's the only difference.
There are trees. Houses of the bourgeois. Doctors, den-
tists, notaries, bank managers, burgomasters.

It was a pleasure to be able to make verbal reports,
in language as brief and colloquial as he cared to
make it. Van der Valk was even quite an almighty
personage here; he could puncture the burgomaster's evening and make any one of fifteen thousand
people shake in his shoes. Which he couldn't do in
Amsterdam!

On the whole, he preferred being a small fish that
looked very small indeed in a very big pond. Still, to
be free of reports was nice. He was accustomed,
heaven bear witness, to written reports—they are
seven-tenths of a policeman's life. He was even good
at them, but he'd never got over detesting them.

He was received by the burgomaster's wife, a pretty
woman, a bit artificially blond. With the wrong
make-up she would have looked thoroughly vulgar,
but she had been very careful with clothes and face
and voice. Lady of the manor, but ever so unspoiled
and charming when receiving flowers from little girls.
He instantly saw her cutting the ribbon for the orphanage's new wing, and did not care greatly for her.
She looked at him as though he were a lavatory at-
tendant, drunk on duty, at that.

"I'm afraid you cannot— You must ask for an appointment in writing." Van der Valk supposed it was
the maid's day off.

"Just give him my card, if you will be so good." He
still got a disapproving look for not knowing his place,

and he watched her walk away with more pleasure. Clothes a bit offensively Christian, but nice legs and a certain allure from the back. Van der Valk, he thought, blow your nose, and avoid lechery.

The burgomaster appeared, in rather self-conscious television undress of tweed jacket and woolly slippers.

"Of course, of course. Er—I'm sorry, Ansje, this is business of importance, and confidential. Come into my study—er, Mr. Van der Valk."

He fussed a little, wondering whether to be genial, or whether to be the superior official, on the cold side. Decided to be genial. More tactful.

"Er—perhaps a glass of sherry?"

"Many thanks."

"There we are. And—what progress have you made so far? I realize these are early days. Is your house adequate, by the way?"

"Yes, thank you. Your admirable secretary filled all the gaps and even got some things my wife forgot. I was most grateful to her."

"Ah, yes, Miss Burger's splendid—admirable is the word. She knows how to get hold of anything. So— you're not too dissatisfied with your start?"

"Sure I'm dissatisfied."

"Oh." The wind was taken out of the municipal sails, a scrap. "But you've reached some fruitful conclusions? Suspects, for instance. You've succeeded in isolating some suggestive uh, discoveries?"

"There aren't any suspects, so I can't isolate any. Unless you mean in the sense that everyone is suspect, even yourself."

"Ah—quite."

"I'm isolating victims. Indeed, the author of these crimes, disturbances—call it what you will—is a victim. Someone unable to resist pressure."

"I hope"—earnestly—"you're not in danger of taking an overly—what shall I call it?—metaphysical viewpoint, Inspector? When can we all be assured that a solution will be found? I do agree that the mental state of this uh, author will give psychiatrists a headache. But is that the most fruitful ground for your approach?"

"I haven't any approach. But everybody spent months hunting for suspects—I still think there's more to be learned from the victims."

"Can you give me no concrete reassurances, though, based on what you've seen and done these—three, isn't it?—days?"

"Certainly. We'll soon run this amorous letter writer to earth, burgomaster. You can be reassured. And I don't even think the field of inquiry will prove to be so very large. Further than that I would not like to go yet."

"Excellent. By the way, have you yourself formed any opinion about our friend Besançon?"

"Yes, indeed. I've met him. I like him very much."

"You don't think yourself that he's involved in any way?"

"Not for a minute. Except that he's a victim, too, of course."

"I suppose so. Naturally, that terrible history would lead anybody into feeling deep sympathy for such a man, and yet—who knows what goes on in a man's head who has seen the things he has?"

It was the first sensible remark Van der Valk had heard from him, and he looked at the burgomaster with proper respect.

6

"How did you get on?" Arlette asked sympathetically.

"Oh, I smeared him with jam. When he got jam on his eyelids and between his fingers, and couldn't pester me any more, I shoved a bit down his throat and left him to enjoy it. He's all right—only wants reassurance."

"I'm glad to see you're feeling better."

"I go around like Father Brown, being enigmatical and paradoxical. And now I could do with a drink. I got thimblefuls of sherry doled out to me."

Van der Valk felt he was not, happily, the least like James Bond. He didn't have hanging locks of hair, he didn't kill people (not, that is to say, quite so many), he wasn't very British, and he was left unmoved by passionate women with eccentric names. But he did like large cold expensive drinks in large cold expensive glasses. Here's to you, Bond, he thought. May your sexual capacities never grow less. But do be careful, old boy. Don't ever tap yourself on the head with the emerald Fabergé spoon, thinking you're a boiled egg in a four-and-a-half-liter Bentley eggcup.

"You ought to get that Miss Burger to see about finding me a refrigerator," said Arlette. "Don't eat all the salt biscuits—I haven't had any yet."

Arlette walked toward the town hall, stopping every time something interested her. Flowers: a good deal dearer than at home, she noted with disapproval. Children's shoes: she had been conscience-stricken at leaving both her boys a little down at the heel. She had to remind herself, too, to look out for a grocer: she had a red cabbage for today, but wanted a reinette apple to go with it.

Men looked at her; women looked at her. The men saw a figure that was striking, if you looked carefully, only because she walked upright and easily on her high heels. Dutch women have a tendency to walk stooped forward, with an inelegant lurch, as soon as they get up on high heels.

There was nothing remarkable to look at about her. She wore her hair up, showing the nape of a nice neck. She was average height and width, fair, with a slightly pale face, strong bony features that were quick and nervous, a nose that could not quite be called Roman. Now, why did the men turn around? It bothered her slightly; it was not especially to gloat over her, for though there was admiration there, certainly, there was a good deal of heavy suspicion, as though she were probably a spy. Her clothes were sober; there was nothing exaggerated about her walk—why did the eyes cling so?

The women saw plain black leather shoes, darkish stockings, a coat that was light for a northern winter, with a rather mean amount of Canadian squirrel to decorate it, and a black beret with Arlette's diamond brooch in it. That sounded quite grand, but it had been her mother's; an old-fashioned Victorian spray of apple leaves and blossom. It had been mended several times, and the diamonds were dirty but undisputable.

She had a black calf bag, black leather gloves from Czechoslovakia (a great bargain and a good cut), and sunglasses.

Was it perhaps the sunglasses? Arlette, like many women (it is noticeable how many Dutch women wear spectacles), found the hard gray light more of a strain on her eyes than sunshine. She had always tended to get wrinkles around the eyes, and the glasses —which weren't very dark, really—did help. But she was puzzled. The men looked suspicious, but the women looked downright hostile. She felt a slight sense of hurt, for she was basically a gentle person with a strong need of being liked and a good capacity for making friends. She had thought her clothes and manner unobtrusive, and quite correct for the wife of a responsible civil servant. And so they were.

The man behind the glass window of the Information counter could see her perfectly well; indeed, he kept staring at her over the shoulder of the man he was talking to, with an eye at once owlish and impudent, as though wishing to undress her but not quite knowing how to go about it. But he made no move at all to ask what she wanted; he just left her standing there, and she tapped her foot irritably—officials of the pettier sort are the same in France, Poland, or Outer Mongolia (which must be, she had decided, rather like this). At last, after inquiring at the greatest possible length into the health of all the other man's brothers-in-law, he stumped unwillingly over toward her.

"Good morning," Arlette said. He didn't bother about the good mornings.

"Well?" he said loutishly.

"Where can I find Miss Burger, please?"

"What d'you want with Miss Burger?" That was just the kind of thing that put cayenne in her mouth.

"What can that possibly have to do with you?" she said with a strong accent.

"Room twenty-four," grudgingly. "Up the stairs." His back was already turned.

Arlette's sense of hurt deepened, even though she was accustomed to the universal extreme rudeness of the public servant. She tapped at the door of Room 24.

"Come in," called a clear soft voice.

"You are Miss Burger—I hope? I'm Mrs. Van der Valk." The woman who sat behind the desk, in a tidy pleasant office with winter sunlight in it, got up at once, taking off her glasses, with a very nice smile that comforted her.

"Oh, I'm delighted. Do please come in and sit down." The voice was warm, and made Arlette's voice sound hard and metallic, so that she softened it as much as she could and said, "I hope I'm not disturbing you."

"Not a bit; the burgomaster's gone to Emmen for a meeting."

In the corner of the office were two plastic-leather office armchairs and a round glass-topped table. Arlette sat on one; Miss Burger sat on the other and leaned forward with a winning, confidential look, like a female psychiatrist.

Miss Burger might have been two or three years on either side of forty. She had soft curly hair cut simply and quite short, and very well brushed; it gleamed with health and was a lovely *feuille-morte* color. She had pale clear skin, fine greenish-brown eyes, straight well-shaped features, and a chin that was only a scrap too long. She wore no make-up at all, which suited her. In a lamb's-wool twin-sweater set her figure was slim and her throat unwrinkled. Her hands were sturdy, with short strong nails, like those of a very good housewife. No rings; no jewelry at all.

She gave her skirt a flip and crossed her legs as though to take dictation, and Arlette realized with a tiny shock something she had seen but not grasped when the woman got up. Miss Burger was two sizes bigger below the waist, so that her lower half seemed to belong to a different woman altogether. Broad hips were draped in one of those unbecoming skirts cut up into a multitude of fussy little pleats. Her legs were heavy, with coarse hair on the calves. Her feet were large and she had made everything from the knee down even worse with lumpish cuban-heeled shoes, dark blue, with bad large buckles on the instep.

"Do tell me how you are getting on. I apologize for that furniture; I'm only too aware of what a haphazard lot it all is. But there wasn't any budget for it, you see. We got that house by a kind of accident and furnished it whatever way we could."

"Oh"—Arlette was wishing to apologize herself by this time—"I think it's fine, really. Just those curtains in the living room."

"Oh, I know," cried Miss Burger with very emphatic glowing warmth. "The horrid things don't fit. They were made for another house altogether whose windows were three inches smaller. I'm ashamed."

"No, no," protested Arlette awkwardly. "They're a little bit skimpy perhaps, but we won't die on that account."

"Do tell me whether there's anything you want."

"Well, yes, perhaps. Just the kitchen—I haven't anywhere to keep food very much."

The Dutch say "yust." Arlette, who had never quite learned how to do this, said "shust." Miss Burger's warm smile had something almost protective about it.

"I wondered if you could tell me where I could perhaps hire a refrigerator?"

"Hire? Good heavens, it would cost a fortune. Now, just let me think a minute."

She thought, tapping on her strong front teeth with the ballpoint she had, through habit, kept in her hand. "I know," she said. "There's a shop in the town that bought up a lot of rather horrid refrigerators. They have cheap nasty plastic inside that crackles and breaks easily. He can't get rid of them— especially as we aren't really refrigerator-conscious here." The smile flashed. "We'll make him give us one cheap. Don't worry; I can get our secretary to sign a chit for that. I'll phone the man right now. Their one merit is that they're large; you'll be able to put away everything." She was already dialing.

"Hello, Jaap? Burger here," in a no-nonsense tone. "Listen . . ." She switched suddenly into the local language, a Dutch that is not a true dialect, but more a matter of vowels pronounced differently, and different word endings, a different intonation. It is about as difficult to follow, for somebody Dutch, as Tennessee hillbilly would be to a Boston Republican. Arlette, the immigrant, could not follow it, and had already felt foolish in the shops on that account. But she got the last phrase, delivered with strong emphasis. "And this afternoon before five, you understand me, Jaap?"

"Otherwise," she added to Arlette, putting the phone down, beaming with the warmth that was so unexpected in that building, "he'll start remembering it two weeks from now."

"You are kind."

"Not a bit. What I'm here for, to smooth paths. You're sure there's nothing else while we're at it?"

"No, truly." Arlette secretly had several other things, but was ashamed to mention them; it would have seemed ungrateful.

"Do you go to church?" asked Miss Burger very suddenly and startlingly.

"Well, yes," stammered Arlette, much embarrassed. "I am Catholic, you see."

"Oh, of course. Forgive me; stupid of me not to have guessed. Yes . . . Well, you must come and see me again. And be sure to tell me if there's anything at all I can do. I told your husband the same; I do hope he realized that I was in earnest. I know how these surveys can run aground on matters that are really quite accessible if only one knows where to look."

Arlette realized suddenly that she was being dismissed. She had liked Miss Burger, but she walked back to the house in the Mimosastraat a good deal puzzled. Once there, she found with annoyance that she had forgotten the apples.

7

Van der Valk woke up in deep gloom and knew it was going to be one of those days. The coffee was revolting, the weather beastly, the windshield wipers were on the blink all day, and when he got home, Arlette had forgotten (a) to put the trash can out, (b) that it was early closing day.

Still, that was all unimportant. Things like this happened to Rembrandt, too. What worried him the whole day was not understanding a damn thing about provincial towns in Drente. Served him right. Puffed up with braggadocio, thinking all the other policemen were imbeciles. The elaborate disguise, the calculated politenesses and rudenesses, the vaunted urban sophistications . . . POOH

He was a vain, prattling dolt

He knew nothing

He understood nothing.

When you meet the unorthodox, meet it in an unorthodox way. Pooh—with froth on top.

He was sitting in M. Cousteau's bathyscaphe, exploring the great silent wonders of the submarine world. Suddenly he noticed a signboard—neat white paint on shiny blue enamel. Very common in Holland.

"You are now standing at the exact geographical center of the Gobi Desert," it said admonishingly. "No admittance for unauthorized persons (Article 436 of the Code of Criminal Law)."

He looked out of his copperbound crystal window. Damn it, they were dead right. He was out of his depth, he told himself wittily.

He went home and was curt with Arlette, till she got fed up with it.

"Look, I agree that we've both eaten better meals, but there's nothing wrong with this dinner, even if it is mostly out of boxes. Will you please stop being disagreeable—or at least tell me what's wrong with you? You're depressed, I can see— Why don't you tell me?"

"Because I make it a rule not to, as you know very well, and also because you dislike intensely hearing about these things."

"Listen. We're together here. We're alone. This place, this house, whatever it is, has been wished on me as well as on you." She thought hard. "We're just going to stack these dishes. Sit down over there. Pour me out a glass of Ashtray." This was her name for a sort of German marc whose full title goes "Asbach Uralt Is-the-Soul-of-the-Wine." Being French, she felt it her duty to be comic about this, but he noticed she enjoyed drinking it.

He heard Arlette put all the dirty dishes in the sink, then heard her go upstairs, change her frock, comb her hair, repair her paint, and go to the lavatory.

Not only was he unaccustomed to the lack of privacy in a small suburban house, but he was outraged at the loss of dignity it implied. The whole street, he thought viciously, can hear and apparently has to know every detail of my wife's everyday existence. Things that aren't even my business. I find this revolting.

She had changed into a wool frock, a soft dusty buttercuppy color that he was fond of. She smelled good; he wished, as he did every day, that he could give up smoking and get a better nose. Taste things, and deposit them politely in a silver spittoon. A tea blender —that would make a splendid job for Van der Valk.

"I hate crimes, yes," she said, holding the lighter up to the cigarette in her mouth. "Hate murders, and all the ghastly gory details. But I can't really see that whatever's been going on here is much of a crime."

"If you put moral pressure on people till they feel there's no way out but to kill themselves, it's as much of a murder as a plastic bomb."

"I suppose so, yes. But isn't it society that is the murderer more than the person? Environment or whatever it is? If I've understood, people killed themselves for fear of the public, for fear of newspapers, what people will say. . . . In other words, they couldn't stand the pressure of existence. What difference is there to someone who commits suicide because of an unhappy love affair—the girl who is pregnant and feels abandoned by everybody, say? The man who drinks and can no longer keep a job—or—oh, anything. Go on, tell me."

"You are my resource against depression, aren't you?" He was touched.

"And isn't that my job?"

"I find you a thoroughly nice woman."

"Now, tell me—what is getting you down?"

"Being a foreigner. I've never felt so conscious of it in my life. Not in France or even England."

"You? But I'm a foreigner. You're the one who's Dutch. Sometimes you're even very Dutch," grinning.

"Not here." Van der Valk: one deep sigh.

A drink of Ashtray lent him some sort of spurious energy. "I came across a file of reports. Brief notes on

police-court cases, annotated by a judge. Pointing out
that people from this part are emigrants in Holland—
in the metroland. I mean, our way. They're still in
their own country, but they're strangers. They seem to
have a higher percentage of petty indictments brought
against them than the home product. This judge
formed a theory, and wrote a memo on it to the Ministry. That they feel both inferior and lonely. Deduc-
tion, the indictments are due to a sort of crude
bravado—compensation feelings. You follow?"

"I follow, but I'm not sure I understand."

"Simply that this is a foreign country. When people
from these parts get south, say, of Amersfoort, they
find that nobody understands their language, the food
is different, the ideas are different, there are Catholics
and all sorts of other riffraff around, and they are
looked at as having crawled straight out of the bog. But
here the boot is on the other foot. We're the rotten
foreigners; they resent us and they kick. Every way
they can. They cheat, even—I've been diddled out of
nickels a dozen times already."

"I've noticed that but I thought they were penny
pinchers because they were poor."

"*Que,* poor."

"They've been terribly poor for generations. One
doesn't get it out of the blood so quickly."

"I don't believe it. I think one forgets quick enough,
and they're all dripping with it now."

"The ground has a lot to do with it. Bad ground.
Just like in the Haute-Savoie."

"I don't think that's quite everything. It's a religious
thing, too. These queer parts of countries are different
in more ways. You look at the figures Larousse gives

for the different *départements* of France on cases of alcoholism, mental disease, congenital deformity, as well as the poverty diseases like T.B. There's a sharp jump upward in the backwoods territories—Savoie, Morbihan, parts of Languedoc. Same here, I'll bet. I think they feel apart; they feel persecuted, and feel hatred for the occupying army. Why should strangers come here and get rich? Skin them every chance you get. Skin the brethren, too, by all means, but that's part of the game—they know the rules. But common front against the outsiders. Of course, there are more and more outsiders, and they can't go on forever, but they're keeping up a rear-guard action."

"You're feeling that."

"And how."

"Are the people who suffer from the nasty letters strangers?"

"It's an interesting point; I'll have to study it. But I can't find out how many people have had letters. They won't open their mouths unless I happen to know a way of twisting their arm. Sometimes I get the feeling that all the accusations are imaginary—no basis behind the whole thing."

"Tell me."

"I mean that I think the author of the letters is just making a witch hunt. Popular hysteria feeds on this, and everyone is now ready to believe the worst of anybody and everybody. If the burgomaster, to take an example, now got letters accusing him of something frightful or just shameful—with no atom of truth in it at all—people would make an outcry against him. It's explosive. That's why I've got to stop it. You can feel that people are jumpy, uneasy. Ready to throw accusations, and listen to them seriously. At anyone, however respected. Like at Salem. Did you read that book?"

"*The Devil in Massachusetts*? Yes, fascinating."

"There wasn't any witch, but they constructed dozens. Teen-age girls saw and heard and felt witches all over the place."

"The people had very hard dreary lives, and a rigid Puritan code of ethics."

"See any resemblance?"

"Yes, I suppose so. But as far as I could see, the girls just invented witches to make life more amusing and exciting. They had no newspapers, no radio, television, trains, shops, cinemas. They've all that here."

"Yes, but that's not quite what I meant. Those girls had a vague but strong feeling of guilt, that anything exciting and amusing was caused by the Devil and therefore witchcraft. There were witches, in the people's minds. There I think the parallel is better."

"They hung a lot of innocent people to get rid of the feeling of themselves being guilty—the fear of becoming witches themselves, or even already being witches."

"Exactly. By the girls' accounts, every damned last one of them was a witch. They weren't having that, of course."

Van der Valk found himself enthusiastically pouring another drink and discovered that he had forgotten his depression. Arlette's therapy.

"It's something, though, that they need to cure locally. To call in an outsider, like me—it's a mistake.

They made a resolute common front against me here."

"There's witchcraft on the unspeakable milk here, all right," remarked Arlette frivolously.

8

In the middle of the night he got an idea. The whole street, he had thought indignantly, could hear and apparently had to know every detail of his wife's daily existence.

Why shouldn't he—or his wife—turn the tables? Take a passionate interest in the whole street's daily existence. The way they did themselves. Shadow watching and all the rest.

He could certainly sit all day bird watching with a pair of binoculars, just the way the letter writer apparently did. Like dirty old men in parks. Fascinating—something he had always wanted to do.

He recalled a visit he had once paid to an English wartime comrade, who lived in Bristol. The friend had gone to Cambridge after the war and was now an architect. An intelligent, delightful man, he complained about the dreadful provincialism of Bristol, but admitted that the huge wooded park at the north side—The Downs, they called it—was wonderful.

"Wonderful place for lover watching," he had said amusedly. "We have a little park in the town, too. It's nothing—just a sort of bare hill. For some extraordinary reason the lovers there are quite shameless. The local boys have a perfect name for it."

"What is it?" Van der Valk had been fascinated.

"They call it 'Taking a piece up Mutton Tump.' "

"Mutton Tump?"

"You Dutch. Etymology is really quite simple. 'Tump' is a genuine old word for a small bare hill of some sort. 'Mutton'—have you forgotten already that in the army we used to say, of such-and-such a girl, nurse, Waaf, whatever she was, 'That one hawks her mutton'?"

Mutton Tump! Van der Valk had been enchanted.

The trouble was that he simply didn't have time. In Amsterdam he could have called on an auxiliary. Here he was alone. These middle-of-the-night ideas, he thought, falling asleep again; they never do stand up.

9

"'Are you really interested?" he asked at breakfast. Good coffee this morning; the sun was shining, too.

"I almost think I am."

"Would you like to help me?"

"How on earth can I help you?" She was astonished. What did she know about crimes—or witches, come to that.

"You can help me a great deal."

"But what can I do?"

The Mimosastraat is Holland, and this particular Mimosastraat is Drente.

"I want you to be one of the housewives who spend all day looking out of their windows."

"I'm more likely to be canonized as a second Jeanne d'Arc."

"Yes, I know, but that's all wrong. We are just making them more suspicious of us. Have you exchanged a word with any of them?"

"A distant good morning."

"You see? Now we're reacting by being defensive. Wrong tactics. You don't have to be pally, but talk to them, gossip with them. I don't ask you to invite them all in to drink coffee and to borrow the lawn mower, but don't be stiff or stuck-up. Let them find out you're human even if you are a queer French cow. Talk about the washing and the dusting and the price of cabbage. And, above all, watch. Watch every slightest tiny little thing. And listen. However poisonous, malicious, idle, or stupid it seems to be, hang on to it and write it down; it may prove to be exactly what I want.

"You know"—thoughtfully, holding out his cup for more coffee; in the early morning, thoughtfulness depends a good deal on coffee—"I'm supposed to be making an ethnographic study. I may as well take that quite seriously. The better I play the part, the sooner we'll be out of this."

"I'll do my best," dubiously. "I can't see myself exchanging jollities with the wives over the clothesline, our mouths full of clothespins. But I don't have much to do, with the boys not here, and I can sit with a little notebook."

"You'll be surprised how easy it is. Remember, they'll be bursting with curiosity about you."

Arlette didn't find it difficult. She trotted out shortly with her clothespins, and smiled agreeably at the nearest wife, busily pinning, a back garden away. This was a brisk person, with the quick nervous movements of the housewife, sharp eyes behind her glasses, and a penetrating voice. She responded instantly with the classic gambit "Lovely day for drying."

Arlette found her abominably nosy, a master of the

point-blank question that is rude anywhere else, but
not in Holland.

But she was just as ready to give confidences. It is
indeed the hallmark of the suburban street neither to
have secrets from your neighbors nor to find sharing
theirs at all unusual. Arlette was cross-examined
closely. She forced herself to be voluble about her
children, the horrors of other people's furniture, the
income and pension of government functionaries, and
the utter wickedness of adding yet another cent to the
retail price of margarine. In return she heard all about
the daughter who was a nurse, the daughter still at the
"household school," and the boy who was the same
age as Arlette's eldest— Oh, these boys. Difficult.
French or not, they had plenty of common ground.

Mrs. Tattle, as Arlette christened her promptly,
finished the delicate work of pinning up her husband's
Sunday white shirt, leaned burly mottled arms across
the fence, and told blissfully all about the neighbors
for a quarter of an hour, oblivious to the plaintive
whistle of her kettle in the kitchen telling her it was
time for a nice cup of instant coffee.

10

Van der Valk spent a busy day detecting—things like
having his hair cut, a really long and comforting chat
with a nice woman in a cigar shop, another with a
bored functionary in the Labor Bureau (with full employment he had nothing to do these days). This way
he was piecing bits of his puzzle together. There
seemed to be nothing wrong with his disguise; he had
grown more and more daring, and had penetrated

such sanctums as the local bureau of the Income Tax Inspectorate, the Ministry of Social Affairs, and the adjutant of the local police force, on the pretext that he was interested in working permits recently issued for Turkish laborers in the building trade. (All the Dutch laborers popped over the border to Germany every week, coming home on Friday nights with a pay envelope twice the size of the one they got in Holland; a thorn in the flesh, this, of both Tax Inspectorate and Social Affairs.)

Nobody, not even the adjutant—a shrewd enough chap, too—guessed that he was a policeman. None of them had any real work to do, and all were delighted to find that a superior official from the Ministry of the Interior had little to do, too, that he liked nothing better than a quiet natter, and that he had not, apparently, come to disturb their repose. They were all friendly bureaucrats together, Masonic, Machiavellian, and determined that whatever they did, it would take a minimum of one year to do it, because no problem is Unimportant.

But few of these folk were from Drente. Like all government officials, they were posted hither and yon at the whims of their superiors, and their opinions of Zwinderen, while illuminating, were not very helpful. Van der Valk wanted to get close to the local people, and it was just that which was so difficult. He knew now the silence that would fall in any haunt of the real natives if he put his nose in at the door.

He got disgusted toward the middle of the afternoon with being a functionary and went to develop his theories in Mr. Besançon's company.

"You are an expert in being a suspected stranger.

Not only a foreigner but a conjurer. In other centuries you would undoubtedly have been denounced as a witch. In this century you are simply suspected of writing obscene letters."

Besançon smiled behind his table, where he habitually sat. It was a big, very old table, of ordinary softwood, put together by some local carpenter. Its legs were not turned, but rounded roughly by eye with a spokeshave; its broad top was marked and scored by tools, hands, use, wear. A good table, and he sat there comfortably at it, as much of a king as a minister behind some pompous mahogany twirlygig in Carlton House Terrace. When he spoke or listened, his hand often passed over the wood, as though he got pleasure from the sturdy outlines. Van der Valk liked that; he would have done the same, perhaps.

"It is largely my fault," slowly. "My doing, then. I avoid contact, I bury myself behind my wall, I have outlandish ways."

"Has the wall any special significance?"

"It is an anachronism, which I accepted gratefully. A century ago, I suppose it kept the lunatics in and deprived the public of a good stare. It still does. I lived for so long in public—I asked for nothing better. But a wish for privacy is always distrusted; seek it and they think you wish to be rude."

"Ha. I have noticed."

"I do not think of it as a protection from a hostile world. It has no mental significance to me. Simply a high blind wall to keep out the curious and the prying. I admit that I sought it out, that I enjoy it. Deliberately, you might even say, I erected it."

"A high blind wall. Uh. Mine is not blind—a glass wall. But I can neither hear nor speak. A deaf wall."

"It worries you."

"Very much. You see, if I am any good at my job at all, it is because as a rule I am quick to make contact with people. I talk freely to them, and tempt them into being as free with me. Then I can feel them, smell them, taste them. I'm halfway then to understanding. Without that I can never get far. This business has confounded policemen who know more about the local people, who are probably cleverer than me. Since I don't understand, how can I get anywhere?"

"There are any number," said Besançon slowly, "of things in the world—often tragic, even terrible—one does not understand, and one never will. The human being stands there helpless, at a loss, often terrified."

"That is true." Van der Valk found himself thinking of the children with leukemia, the clinic in Corsica; he had read about it a week or so before in *Paris Match*. The professor in Paris said, "Sir, your cure is worthless." The Corsican peasants said. "Give every child a chance." Who was right? Both, obviously.

"Is this affair really so important?"

"Not a bit, relatively. The prevalence of road accidents is much more important. To me it is—first, because it's my job to stop this kind of thing; second, because I got sent here specially, told point-blank that the others had been flummoxed but that I'd better not be. I need to win this one; otherwise I'll stay a post-office counter clerk my entire life.

"And it does have a certain importance, all the same. Not so much in the death of two women, but an attitude of mind that is all wrong, and that I think is the underlying cause. A certain parallel with persecuting Jews."

"This I don't follow," said Besançon politely. Van der Valk realized that he was gibbering.

"I mean that this is perhaps a small unimportant example of something we see everywhere. A mass hysteria that grows out of a mass self-deception, a mass neurosis. There is something wrong with life— blame it on a handy scapegoat. Jews, Communists, Negroes, Cubans—you name it, we've got it in stock. Here, so my feeling is running, there's a tendency to hate strangers. As though they were saying, 'We were perhaps poor, but everything was all right till you came along.' I am afraid I'm probably exaggerating this. Very likely I am. But, so far, it's all I've got."

Besançon asked, suddenly, the same question Arlette had asked.

"And these people who have received letters—were they strangers?"

"I've no idea. I don't think so, particularly. But I've no real idea because I'm never likely to find out just who has had letters. But don't misunderstand me. It's not a real physical parallel. The letters haven't any nigger-go-home angle. Just that I get a sense of community that is tight and closed against outsiders, and a little unimportant internal upset like this has a destructive effect that may become serious. What causes the disruption?"

"Your interest in Jews—you simply think that whatever was wrong with the Germans, they tried to make a scapegoat of the Jews."

"I suppose that seems obvious enough; it's very broad. I couldn't narrow it much. I know nothing about Jews and precious little about Germans."

"So you're not drawing a parallel. You're taking a vague idea as an illustration."

"Yes." Van der Valk wondered why the point seemed so important to him. He had only brought it up, as he said, as a vaguely illustrative notion.

"Perhaps I'm making a mistake. You have only to correct me if that is so. You come to me—and you are very welcome—and you give me confidences, almost."

"That's true. It's a way I have."

"It wouldn't be a scheme, would it—quite a carefully arranged scheme?"

"To pretend to confide in you, as though spontaneously? With what object? To incriminate you?"

"It has been known."

"I see that you know quite a lot about policemen." He smiled.

"I wouldn't be above it if I thought it necessary. Should I suspect you of something?"

"I am no judge of that. I have been suspected of so many things."

"You are sensitive."

"I have been interrogated by many, many policemen in my day. Perhaps now I put myself, as it were, automatically in the position of suspect."

"I came, quite frankly, having found somebody intelligent, to pick his brains."

He smiled again. "What I have is at your disposal."

Van der Valk changed the subject. There was no use in pursuing it.

11

Arlette, when he got home, was watching for him. She had taken his instructions, his silly plan, very seriously, and had filled four pages of one of his scratchpads with pure ethnographic research, quite trivial and absurd, and probably very valuable. He could turn it all over to a sociologist from Yale University making a survey of provincial towns. Like the man who wrote the absorbing book about the status seekers. He read all her notes carefully while she stood like a self-conscious schoolgirl having her essay corrected.

"One thing happened that was unusual. I didn't know how to put it down briefly. I thought I could tell you if you were interested; you can judge for yourself. I'm probably imagining things right away—I knew I'd be no good at this."

"Tell me."

"Housewives' snooping—incredible. If I lived here, I'd turn into a windowpeeper, too." She was indignant with herself.

"Tell me, then."

"It's nothing, really, and in Amsterdam I would have paid no heed at all, if I'd even noticed, which I probably wouldn't. And I wouldn't have listened. Here I did listen—avidly."

He had to laugh. She wasn't only indignant; she was ashamed of herself.

"Woman. Stop tantalizing. Nothing is important, but observe whatever you see with total accuracy. You never know, you may discover the long-sought cure to the common cold."

"Well . . ." Plunge. "A couple down the road had a fight. Three doors down across from us. That's—let's see—number ten. There's a man and his wife and they have a little girl, about five, with long hair tied in a bow with a ribbon."

"I'm trying to place them in my mind."

"He has a little beige car, sort of butty-looking."

"I know—Fiat eleven hundred. I've got him. I think he's a traveler in drinks and things."

It amused her, and slightly horrified her, that he was paying attention. That he had his notebook out, and had written on top of a clean page, "Mimosa-straat. No. 10. Beige Millecento." She was a witness; he was taking down her information. He could see that she felt this to be a bit immoral after twelve years of being married to him.

"I've learned a good deal of miscellaneous gossip about the whole street."

"You tell me everything in order. Continue with the row."

"The first I heard was when I was ironing in here and heard a door slamming—a front door it sounded like—and a woman's voice screaming 'Peter! Peter!' So I remembered what you told me and flew to the window—I may say that every wife in the street did exactly the same. The auto door banged, too; that was the man—Peter, I take it—getting in. She flew out after him, got into the car just as it started, and there seemed to be a sort of struggle inside, because the auto lurched all over the street. I suppose she was hanging on to the steering wheel, but I couldn't see properly"—conscientious. "Anyway, it stopped down the street, out of my sight." She went a bit pink. "I went to the door and looked. You did tell me."

"You weren't the only one, I'll bet."

"If I hadn't gone, I'd have been the only one. But I thought myself a dirty bitch, standing there blissfully enjoying someone else's private troubles. It was a very suburban scene. I mean, here everything seems so hidden and hushed up, and therefore everybody peeks. At home nobody looks because they don't seem ashamed—people do often have fights on the pavement, after all. When they aren't ashamed, one doesn't feel ashamed oneself. Remember Mrs. Brooks, the grocer's wife, in her nightie, racing down the street at three in the morning screaming 'Put down that black thing!' We did so wonder what she meant."

"Everybody looked then, too."

"Only because she made such a racket she woke us up—and I did wonder about the black thing—and because I hated Brooks; slimy man, wanting to rape one if he as much as sold half a pound of carrots."

"Dear Mrs. Brooks—extraordinary clothes she wore. But we're digressing. Back to Peter."

"They'd come to a standstill and were having an argument, but I couldn't make the words out. He got out then, and seemed about to walk on, but she ran after him and clung. She kept on saying 'Peter, Petter!' "

"What time was all this?"

"About three; all the housewives were drinking tea. Half the men in the street are salesmen, or something —one often sees them at home in the afternoons. Well, Peter sort of shrugged her off, and she went down on her knees and clutched his leg. To stop him getting away, it looked like. He turned around—they were at the end of the street—and I suppose he saw a whole row of housewives staring their eyes out, and I dare say that cooled him down. Anyway, he suddenly turned back toward the house. She went after him, and tried to hang on again. You could see she was really in a state; she didn't care who was looking. Just in front of the door of their house she started clutching again, and I think he suddenly got mad because he gave her a real wallop. I bet she has a black eye. That snapped the tension; he just took hold of her and brought her in and shut the door. There wasn't any more. Just silly, but I did think I ought to tell you."

"Quite right, because I'm very interested."

"Really, or do you say that to encourage me?"

"No, really. Now, tell me the answers to a few things. Do you think he was mad at her all along? I mean that he walked out because he'd come in and found her in bed with the butcher—or just that he got mad at her making a scene in the street?"

"More that, I think, because he seemed quite calm and controlled till the last moment, when he smacked her—but I could be wrong."

"Did it seem as though she were trying to excuse herself for something she had done, or was supposed to have done?"

"Not really. She had a sort of begging voice—it could have been 'Don't leave me,' or just 'Don't do it' —whatever it was he was wanting to do when he got in the car. Oh, yes, getting in—it took her a moment to get the car door open—she shrieked 'Don't tell it!

Don't tell it!' I've no idea what she could have meant, though—maybe nothing; she was really hysterical."

"Right up my street," with appetite.

Arlette looked a little aghast at being taken seriously.

"And I can't do a damn thing. I think I'm going to yield to a temptation I've always had. I want to get to the bottom of this. I'm going to give the police an anonymous phone call."

"Oh, darling. That's really revolting—do you have to?"

"How else are we to find out? One thing—I don't think I know her to place her. What's she like? Pretty?"

"Well, she's not absolutely horrible," said Arlette charmingly. "About twenty-seven, maybe twenty-five. Huge feet, and seems quite flat-breasted. Sort of bony. Small foxy face, quite pretty I suppose but sort of stupid, like the baker's girl at home—the one on the corner."

Fairly typical Arlette description. It sounded as though the woman were not bad at all. Mm, another young, pretty married woman.

"Listen. This sounds to me like a good example of the type of emotional scene that's being played around here lately more often than one would expect. It might, of course, be nothing at all, but again it might be helpful, and I want to find out. You continue tomorrow—pally tea drinking."

"Oh, that awful Mrs. Tattle—you've no idea. Nosy . . . But she tells as much as she asks, I'm bound to admit. I already know all about her menopause and

Grandpa's hernia, her daughter's boy friend, what stars she's born under—"

"Lovely. But it's important that she doesn't think you too curious. Now I'm going to make my phone call. Amusing, in a sense, that I won't hear for days; I'll have to get a transcript of police interrogations from the burgomaster, sneakily."

Van der Valk didn't have to bother gazing out or peeping through a teeny gap in the curtains himself to know that a police car stopped down the road an hour later.

12

He had thought it comic, making a phone call in a hushed sticky voice, bringing the boys in blue pounding out. Comedy is never far away wherever Van der Valk is operating, our well-known cross-eyed detective with the two left feet. And his intoxicating, cliffhanging certainty of always doing the wrong thing.

But he was quite good at ethnography, he thought with odious self-satisfaction. He was becoming an expert on Zwinderen, and especially on the Mimosastraat. He had masses of poignant information, provided by Arlette's great new friend, Mrs. Prins (a jewel, that woman; he had counted greatly on her), by the milkman, and by his own great new friend, the secretary of the local Good Neighbors' Association. Wonderful fellow, zealous for communal activities and Getting to Know One Another. With enthusiasm, he had shown an admiring Van der Valk all his schemes for social evenings, conversation groups, amateur drama classes, and a splendid notion for sending flow-

ers to every member of the association on their wedding anniversaries.

These Elks and Kiwanis types were, in their own
estimation, a great help to everyone, but they might
have been surprised to discover what a help they were
to him; he picked their brains with delight.

Enchanting to discover all the characters from Sin-
clair Lewis flourishing here forty years after their
time. Babbitt, Will Kennicott, Dr. Almus Pickerbaugh,
the man who knew Coolidge—a Dutch Coolidge;
there are many, and Van der Valk had sometimes
thought that Coolidge's immortal phrase "There exists
no necessity for becoming excited" would make the
ideal motto, graven in letters of bronze outside Ministries, here in Holland.

He had a little map with all the houses of the
Mimosastraat. He looked at it and laughed. A cock-
eyed way of behaving. He hadn't any suspects at all.
He had a little map and a notebook full of gossip and
not one single suspect, not even Besançon.

He knew what Besançon was to him. He was his
confidant, the secret adviser, the *chef de cabinet,* the
power behind the sofa, Father Joseph. It is good when
there is someone like this, someone connected with the
business you are working on, yet somehow outside it.
You can talk to such a person almost with freedom,
sometimes even with friendship. He has character in a
mass of blank shapeless faces; his voice has an individual timbre. Van der Valk recalled many times
when such people had shown him what to do. This
time, he needed a person of that sort more than ever.

He had known, most of those other times, whom he
had been looking for, and why. The trouble had been

proving it without provoking a ghastly drama. He had
always provoked the ghastly drama, having a childish
liking for such things. But here he had nothing to
prove. He had no theories, no hypotheses. The dramas
had already happened; little tiny domestic dramas,
nothing grandiose or lurid. No headlines on this one.
No spectacular interventions or interrogations.

He simply had to stay still, observe, learn. When he
had learned, he would know. The author—as far as
there was an author—would drop off the tree into his
hand. No proving. There wouldn't be anything to
prove. It would all be terribly obvious, and everyone
would say, "But how is it that we never thought of
that?"

The crime—what a word—belonged to the town
where it had happened. An inevitable, inextricable
consequence of a way of life. What were the problems
here that had accompanied the laying of a thin veneer
of glitter, a coating of wealthy materialism, on the old
Calvinist roots of a stick-in-the-mud country market
town?

Arlette, in the intervals of not very determined
housekeeping, roamed about looking out of all the
windows, dutifully, every five minutes at least. The ar-
rival of the milkman seemed to be the great event of
the morning—a rallying sign for all the housewives of
the street to exchange their impressions of the last
twenty-four hours. Her notebook and pencil lay ready,
but she decided that if she wrote down only the things
she felt quite certain of, she would not have much to
put on the page. And if she once began to decorate,
where would it end?

She had been astonished when her husband took
that nonsensical business about Peter-Peter seriously;
she had been extremely ashamed at writing down
those nosed-out trivialities of other people's lives. Her
most immovable tenet of behavior was never to look if
anything embarrassing or humiliating happened to
others in public. Article One was equaled in force only
by Article Two—never let anybody, on any pretext
whatever, have anything to do with your private life—
and that extended definitely to neighbors who wanted
to borrow the lawn mower. Arlette was decidedly not
cut out for suburban existence.

She had not found it easy, ever, in Holland.
Brought up in the French belief that a house is not a
house unless surrounded by a wall six feet high, making your windows, your garden, your back yard as inviolable as your bathroom, she still suffered agonies at
the terrifying nakedness of Dutch life. The sensation
that one was standing on the street in one's under-
clothes, being solemnly, leisurely inspected by everybody who happened to pass—and without anyone,
apparently, ever finding anything the slightest bit ab-
normal about the situation.

Their flat in Amsterdam was in an old house, on
the second floor, with no lift. But even when the children had been tiny, and she had had to lug heavy
wriggling infants up and down, as well as awkwardly
bulging shopping bags, she had always prized the
dusty, unhandy place for its solid soundproof walls, its
small many-paned windows, the sense of two heavy
doors and two long flights of creaking stairs between
her and the street.

How she had always detested her husband's dreadful police habit—that essentially Dutch habit—of stopping anywhere and everywhere for a good unhurried stare into other people's windows.

"See how they've got that plant to grow there, over the sofa," he would remark.

"I don't want to look," she would mutter, squirming.

Never, she had thought, would he really understand. To him, born and bred in Amsterdam, where the street life is as public as that of Naples, it was as natural as breathing for him to look and see how other people lived. Nobody was more deft at inventing reasons for getting right inside, for other people's home, he said often, were the chief ingredient in understanding their characters, all their inner springs and levers. And now, out of loyalty to him, she was trying to teach herself to gaze. It was a kind of treachery; it was painful to her.

He had sometimes suggested trying to find a better flat, even a house. Cheaper, he insinuated, more modern, easier to run. But she had had horrid visions of the mean little strip of grass that is a front garden in Holland, of the mean little hedge (allow it to grow more than waist high and you will get a peremptory letter from the town hall; you risk becoming a traitor to Dutch municipal togetherness), and most of all she dreaded the huge windows that laid bare every carrot you peeled, every spoonful you ate, every polish-smeared rag you applied to your Dutch floor of speckless linoleum.

Since her marriage she had been homesick for the long narrow planks of hardwood, the high stone, the high wrought-iron, the shotgun with which, one second after nightfall, you abolished either the spider or the inspector of police that showed its nose. Oh, *vive la République*.

Perhaps now that he was really in the ugly brick box, staring out at the wet black ground, her dear husband would at last see the point. He had certainly no love for the Mimosastraat. This might, hoped Arlette, cure him of that secret Dutch hankering for the little house with the little garden, which he could dig in when he came home.

PART THREE

FRIENDSHIP

1

VAN DER VALK THOUGHT that there was a streak of fatalism in most policemen. There were so many times when one had no very clear idea how to play one's cards. One threw them down—played them as they lay. He had a labyrinth this time. To save his life he could not have said why he thought Besançon could help him penetrate it. He had nothing whatever to justify their little chats. Perhaps one small thing. It was doubtless out of character, but he agreed with that State Recherche man. There was something strange about the old man, something hidden. Sinister?—no, that was perhaps not quite the word.

He had no idea what the word was.

But why should Besançon have been, all along, Suspect Number 1? The case against him was so very thin. It simply didn't exist. All the policemen, and now he added himself to that distinguished list, had stubbornly gone on thinking that even if Besançon wasn't

guilty of this, damn it, the fellow must be guilty of
something. What?

They hadn't the faintest idea, and no more had Van
der Valk.

He simply could not and would not believe that
Besançon had written those letters. Van der Valk
knew them by heart now. He could quote them from
memory. They were sexy, mm; yes, but only vaguely,
almost inconsequently, as though the writer had
obeyed a conventional feeling that an anonymous letter had to be a bit sexy or nobody would bother reading it; too dull otherwise.

A religious feeling was much stronger in them. Certainly they were very Calvinist. They spoke of God
and the Devil in that characteristically literal, familiar,
glib way. In this person's life, God and the Devil were
very much physically present; looming, almost tangible. Listening, urging, arguing, fighting.

And the other kind of Calvinism, the Coolidge
kind—"Cal for President, Cal for President"—an
overwhelming respectability, conservatism, love of
regulation and formula and bureaucracy; a mincing
muttonhead hatred of risk and innovation.

A local person, Van der Valk was sure by now—or
he thought he was sure—born and bred here, with a
distrust, a dislike, of anything that came from outside.
Cities were spoken of with fear and hatred—strong-
holds of the Devil. An undertone of anxiety. Zwinderen was being invaded by the Devil—the witches of
Salem again—and the Devil must be fought with his
own vile weapons.

There was one odd, perhaps significant fact. The
men who were attacked in the letters were all stran-

gers. The woman—he hadn't checked this yet to a watertight certainty—were all local women. Local— all from this province or the borders of it. This background, this atmosphere. Van der Valk thought there was an unspoken appeal in the letters to them not to play this background false.

Nothing was watertight. Sometimes he thought that maybe ten per cent of the letters had come to light. How could he be sure about anything in them when he hadn't, more than likely, seen a tiny percentage?

Was the writer a woman? There was a feminist streak, and a fear—yes, a hatred—of men. Just men. But was this a convincing argument? He knew feminist men. He was feminist himself. He knew a fellow who carried it pretty far who said that only women make good businessmen—a singularly unpopular point of view in Holland. The fellow even said he could only be friends with women. He was a nice fellow—talked too much but so do others. And the fellow was right in a way—Van der Valk couldn't find himself friends with him but Arlette had.

The fellow had quite a few loose screws. A few more and he could write letters like these.

Besançon had a sort of distrust of women. Van der Valk would have to see if he had any feminist views.

2

He ruminated over Mr. Besançon's homemade bookshelves. Besançon sat at his table, calm and gentle as always. The eyes were very bright and steady behind those dark glasses of his, whatever the vision was like.

"You have the best kind of books," Van der Valk said suddenly.

"Have I? I value them very much, but why should you approve of them?"

"I only meant the books that are read and read till the covers fall off."

"Ah." He smiled. "Have you ever read the memoirs of Aimée de Coigny?" he asked surprisingly.

"No idea even who he is."

"A she, but there's no earthly reason why you ever should have heard of her. She was simply a pretty, adventurous, intelligent woman who was mixed up with many notable persons and events during the Napoleonic time, and left interesting memoirs. She draws a very attractive portrait of Talleyrand in a library, picking up books, 'talking to them as though they were alive.' I like that."

"I can see that you like memoirs."

"To my taste, the only really interesting books. Is it not a strange thing that in the eighteenth century a complete nonentity should write memoirs that are read today with pleasure, whereas today a man whose name is known to all the world writes four hundred pages of the most wearisome sawdust?"

"Today's celebrity is tomorrow's nonentity."

"One wishes always to be either a hundred years ahead of or a hundred years behind one's own time. Nothing can be duller than the present."

Van der Valk sat down and lit a cigar, crossed his hands peacefully upon his ample stomach, gazed at cigar smoke, at Besançon.

Besçanon's stillness was remarkable, untouched by the nervous tremble. There was suspicion in it, the

deep-seated, ever-present wariness of a man who has
spent years in the hands of his enemies, treated with
jocularity and feline cruelty more than with crude bru-
tality. The world to him was nothing but policemen.
No wonder he preferred the eighteenth century, the
century that proclaimed that freedom of thought was
universal, whatever servitude one might be born to. He
could never lose sight of the fact that Van der Valk
might begin again at any moment to persecute him.
How did he stand having the policeman in the house?
Van der Valk knew well enough that he was intrusive.
But this was one aspect of police training—one no
longer cared whether one was intrusive or not.

"I am depressed," Van der Valk said. "I'm not enjoying this job, my own thoughts, my own actions."

He got the smile around the eyes, the slight twitch
of the wide mouth. The deeply sunk facial muscles
hardly moved. Interesting mouth. The lips were thin
and sensitive, but that sensitivity had been held,
clamped taut, for so many years that no emotion would
ever again show there. The lines all around had been
cut in with a chisel and mallet.

"Develop," said the mouth. "Amplify. You wish to
exercise your thoughts—you are a boxer, and I am
your punching ball."

"The job is tedious—but that I am accustomed to.
The pressure to be a pure bureaucrat is great, as always. One wishes for situations that are cut and dried.
For a case out of a textbook or a detective story—cut,
dried, and pigeonholed, too. Everything tidy—the bureaucrat's dream. And they never are. They are in-
variably untidy, sloppy, shapeless.

"Here, too, I must peek and pry, in a way that is

mean and ignoble. These people, these—to me—total foreigners, they resent me, dislike and avoid me. They are quite right. What business have I to come here disapproving of them, laughing at them, holding up their ways to ridicule? I have to do my work, and here I cannot do it without taking away their dignity, without imposing my officially approved norms on their ways, which they've had for years. I am the government, the eternal enemy. I have never felt so strongly how destructive a force that government exerts upon a small provincial settlement, a village geared to village life."

"So you come to me for consolation? To share your solitude with another solitary? You have, unless I gravely misjudge, other motives for your visits."

"I have, yes."

"You see, Insector, you suspect me. Still. Always."

It was so, but Van der Valk was not going to let Besançon cut him with the thin, bitter edge of his amusement over it. Besançon knew well enough that the policeman had no grounds for suspecting him.

"No. That is not what I meant. I think that I come for your advice."

"However dubious I am of its value, I can scarcely refuse."

"Has it ever occurred to you—no, I have phrased this wrongly. Does it ever now occur to you, as a Jew, to feel—now—sympathy with the Gestapo? Understanding, now, can you feel a certain pity? Not for what they did—for them, the men who were your captors and persecutors?"

"Perhaps. Has this some connection with problems of yours?"

"I don't know."

"But let us be factual. As an abstract idea, my answer would be no. In certain circumstances, under certain conditions, I have thought that I understood my captors, as you call them, very well. Even at the time, I often sympathized with them. State your case."

Van der Valk wanted to get up and walk about; he was unaccountably restless and nervous that day. But he had to oppose, he didn't know why, the other's stillness and watchfulness with his own. He felt remarkably young and raw; he had seen that same expression of weary calm on the faces of old policemen in their last years, before they got put out to grass. He had last seen it in Paris, waiting for a taxi in the rush hour outside the Gare du Nord. The agent on duty had the same complete indifference, that of a man who has obeyed orders his whole life, who has seen everything. Everything.

"I am here, possessing administrative and interrogatory powers, in a defeated, occupied land. If I were a simple official who was here to carry out my orders from the central government, openly, honestly, I might feel less uneasy. I would take refuge in my officialdom. I would be the impersonal functionary. Because I am here secretly, anonymously, I do not fit into the pattern, and I lack the security of a formal position. You find me foolish?"

"Not at all. It is an interesting thought."

"These are people whose lives and ideas I find ridiculous, but I find myself, as well, hostile. They hate and fear me. I have a dangerous tendency to despise them, and to believe that their reactionary ways must be rooted out. They are hindrances to progress and opposed to the state administration—a very little more, and I think I would find myself with the mentality of a good Party man. It occurred to me that I would even find myself in sympathy with one of these characters —basically only a policeman like myself, after all— like, say, the notorious Gestapo Müller."

"Ah—Müller." The smile again. "I did not really know the gentleman. I should think that he was difficult to know."

"I should think so, too." Van der Valk grinned back. "A shadowy, opaque individual."

"I dare say I know him as well as most," indifferently. "I do have to admit that I found him quite a reasonable fellow—toward me. I worked, as you obviously know, in his department."

"Oh yes—I've read the long and interesting dossier on you in the archives."

"Yes, indeed. My dossier. Hm. It would not amuse me to see it; I have no doubt that it is a thick useless wastebasket of irrelevant facts and inaccurate conclusions."

"Like most," mildly.

"Indeed. No sillier, I imagine, than the dossier on General Müller."

"That I haven't had the pleasure of seeing."

"I don't think you need worry that there is any striking resemblance between you," said Besançon dryly.

That made Van der Valk laugh. Talking about his neuroses had, as usual, dispelled them. He felt better, which was the whole idea. He wondered vaguely about General Müller. He had been reminded of him

by one of the recurrent three-line sensation items that
are the pepper in the dull stew of a page of newsprint.
Müller had been seen in Nicaragua or somewhere—
yet again.

"I wonder whether he'll ever turn up," vaguely.

"Who cares?" asked Besançon.

"That is one of the surprising facts—so many people still care, and very deeply."

"I don't. Do you?"

"No. Nor do I think he'll ever reappear. I only
thought of a man who, of all things, was a schoolmas-
ter somewhere in the United States. On his deathbed
he said, 'I am Marshal Ney.' There was quite a bit of
evidence—handwriting, and so on. Not conclusive, of
course."

"And do you believe that tale?"

"Of course not. Apart from eyewitnesses, it wasn't in
Ney's character. He had a romantic streak; he wanted
to be sacrificed. He could have escaped much earlier
if he'd wanted—and he wasn't in the least afraid of
death. Why try and run suddenly, just as it became
difficult? No—a romantic legend, I'm afraid."

"I think that General Müller behaved very simi-
larly."

"Just that there were plenty of people who saw Ney
shot. Hell, I have to go and see the burgomaster. He's
a lot duller than you—you'd make a good policeman."

"I'm flattered at your compliment, but the career
does not greatly appeal to me, at my time of life."

"I don't see it surrounded by a rosy glow myself,"
Van der Valk said at the door. "Does it bother you
that I sit here talking nonsense?"

"Not in the least. I may even end by taking an interest in your twists of conscience."

Van der Valk walked over toward the Koninginneweg, mentally rehearsing his report.

3

It was the wife, again, who let him in. Just as unwelcoming as the last time. Regarding him, he thought, with more than disapproval at the husband's being bothered during his free evening by another importunate clown. With suspicion, Van der Valk thought. That's strange. He had two minutes to wait, and amused himself wondering about this completely trivial fact. Why should the burgomaster's wife be suspicious of a functionary from the Ministry of the Interior in The Hague? They are, after all, an integral part of her existence; she must have met dozens. And it is part of her job to be amiable to all of them. This wife, incidentally, was known as a great charmer, most skillful at being amiable to anyone who might be of help in the husband's career. Odd?

Hell, he was going soft in the head. He sat an hour with Besançon, wondering why he was suspicious of him and why Besançon was still so suspicious of him, and he had it on the brain. Here he was imagining that this perfectly harmless woman was suspicious of him; he'd be suspecting her next. Van der Valk will now take all parts previously played by Cary Grant in Alfred Hitchcock films. He's not as old, and even better-looking and he's hell with the women. Van der Valk gazed idly at Madame's bottom disappearing into the living room.

The burgomaster appeared, rather falsely jaunty when he saw his caller; it didn't sound well at all, exactly as though he hated Van der Valk's guts but was putting a good face on.

"Ah, Mr. Van der Valk. Uh—come into the study. I am so sorry, Ansje—but the town's welfare, as usual, comes first." The wife nodded sourly. Sour just because she was enjoying her husband's company? Van der Valk wondered again.

Don't ever start suspecting people, he thought. Every damn person you meet will act suspiciously from then on.

"Well, how is it progressing?"

"It isn't a job, alas, where one can mark progress—so many houses built, so many roads mended—on the little chart that hangs above the desk. I wish it were. We'll go on not knowing for a while longer, and then, quite suddenly, we'll know. And that will be the end of it."

"You really have formed ideas? A certain crystallization? A narrowing of fields?"

"Certainly. There's a shape that makes itself more precise little by little. But it's the shape of a mentality, not a person yet. Our facts aren't complete and we cannot draw conclusions."

"That has always been the drawback. Every investigating officer has said the same thing."

"More facts will turn up. Letters will be written and they won't all be suppressed. We haven't had any for a while, but we are not to conclude from that that the writer just stopped. They don't give up writing. They can't; they must go on till a crisis is reached. They want to reach a crisis."

"But *we* don't. It has caused quite enough trouble already."

"We won't let it get that far. But I'd like it if a few more letters turned up."

"If I follow you, your method has been to build up a hypothetical portrait, and when that is complete, you will search for a person to correspond? I'm not sure I follow."

"I haven't any hypothesis," Van der Valk said woodenly; the fellow was tiresome. "There is a vague similarity to the method of the robot portrait, where a composite photograph is constructed from details given by witnesses. That all needs more psychological knowledge—I haven't any. We're collecting knowledge about the author. Bit by bit. By the way, sir, have you got the transcripts of the police work in the Mimosastraat yet?"

"They aren't complete, but they'll be brought to me tomorrow. You'll have them directly. You think that this woman—or her husband—has had letters?"

"I think that something caused a tension, which boiled over in a street fracas. Something painful, to blind them to the public way they were behaving. Could be letters. I very much want to get hold of more. If this pair correspond to a notion I've formed, it would strengthen my—call it sense of direction. I'd like, for instance, to know whether she is a local woman—and whether he's a local man."

"Miss Burger could find out very easily."

"Would you be kind enough to add a note if it's not already in the file?"

"It has a bearing on your thoughts?" Making a note with a presentation silver pencil.

"A bearing on character. The local people have, to my eyes, strongly marked features—what one might almost call local traits."

"Ah, the local character." The burgomaster smiled. "I had difficulties with it myself when I came; I felt a good deal of an outsider. I was fortunate in that my wife comes from this part of the world. She was the greatest help. She secured, so to speak, my admission. Of course, in any small community the outsider is regarded with suspicion."

"To be sure."

"Well—to summarize—your confidence is not diminished."

"Confidence . . ." Van der Valk had to suppress a grin; it sounded as though the burgomaster were asking for the loan of fifty cents' worth till Monday.

"Believe me, burgomaster, there's no need of it. Patience and concentration. I only wish I were forty feet tall and had a magnifying glass. If I could achieve a minutely accurate observation of everything, I'd have this person for you tomorrow. Everything down to temperature of the outside air. A naturalist—Fabre studying ants." The burgomaster had an expression halfway between the bemused and the disapproving.

"You can't compare human beings to ants, surely."

"Of course not, except in one sense. There's a pressure here on human beings to conform, and not conforming is a thing that's strictly forbidden in antland."

Van der Valk felt he shouldn't have opened his great mouth, but he held his peace. By profession, training, mentality, upbringing, moral belief, the burgomaster would find it difficult to sympathize with Van

der Valk's little ways. But he was intelligent, painstak-
ingly tolerant, and had great respect for ability,
whether it was the minister, Miss Burger, or even the
police. If Van der Valk showed ability, he would be
forgiven the ants.

"I only see one drawback to your exposé. If this—
uh, observation, patience—takes longer than you
count upon, what then?"

"It always does. Never, never can one sit down and
study a peculiar set of circumstances the way I mentioned, like the naturalist. We have to leave that to the
sociologists. Time and the taxpayer who foots the bill
are our big enemies, as you know yourself, burgomaster."

"Only too true, alas."

"Every so often, we just have to take time by the
hair—do something that may be precipitate and seem
ill-judged. I won't bother you any longer, burgomaster."

"You can pick up the report tomorrow afternoon if
you wish. I'll bring it home at lunchtime."

"I'll do that. And many thanks. We're not likely to
get any further deaths, you know."

"I sincerely hope not. You know your way?"

"Yes, thanks, don't bother."

It didn't occur to Van der Valk till he was out the
door to ask the burgomaster something, and by then it
was too late. Had he, Van der Valk wondered, told his
wife that Van der Valk was from the Ministry, or how
had he explained the evening visits? Perhaps he was a
wise man and simply hadn't offered any explanations
at all.

It had got colder. Van der Valk had to walk back to the main road, where he had left the Volkswagen; the wind had veered into the north and strengthened. That will break this mild weather, he thought vaguely, and perhaps will be a good omen. He hated westerly weather. The depression by the Azores, which they talk learnedly about in the weather forecasts, to him just sounded depressing, especially when it was south of Iceland.

"What d'you want?" asked Arlette. "Port or a glass of milk?"

"Port, please. I didn't even get a thimble of sherry from the city father, this time."

"You look happier."

"I suppose I am happier. Not bad port; what did it cost?"

"Bit on the sugary side. About a dollar."

"Weather's going easterly—I feel sharpened. And that old Besançon sharpens me; he's an intelligent old man. I don't feel quite so wound in moist warm blankets."

"Penetrating."

"A tiny bit. Not enough yet. Any more developments down the road?"

"Nothing heard or seen, though I've stared dutifully through the lovely net curtains."

Arlette hated net curtains; she found it a bore having to wash them.

"Nothing more will happen, probably. It doesn't matter; I'll get the police reports tomorrow."

"The neighbors doubtless know. They recognize police a mile off."

"That's just where we're handicapped. If you see a
man step out of an auto and knock at somebody's
door, you think nothing of it. But the neighbors say,
'Aha, she's a week behind with her insurance pay-
ments.' You never can catch up with a place where
everybody knows everybody else."

"Never mind, you feel sharpened."

"Enough, I hope, to see through walls as well as the
next man. What was on the television?"

"Football. One of them lay down and pretended to
be hurt. Footballers get more babyish every day. The
Germans are terribly excited—they've broken some
record or other."

"What record?"

"Truly, I haven't the faintest idea. Is it important?"

"Not at all."

"Hell, I've let the milk boil over again."

4

Van der Valk drove past the burgomaster's house, up
the Koninginneweg, the road favored by the prosper-
ous of the little town: the thriving shopkeepers, the
senior executives of the factories. A straight, broad
road, as nearly settled as could be found in the whole
raw, self-conscious community. The houses—half of
them, anyway—had been there ten years and were just
beginning to weather. The shrubs in the trim front gardens were filling out; the grass was losing its newly
planted look.

At the bottom of the main street, facing the canal,
there were grand houses, too. All who were patrician

in the village had always lived on the Willemsdijk, in tall nineteenth-century houses with gables and painted woodwork, stained-glass windows and wrought-iron work on the front door. Here had lived the burgomaster, the notary, the advocate, the doctor, and the vet. One or two were still there, steeped in solid gloomy grandeur. Good wood and not much light; velvet curtains a bit musty; tiled hallways decidedly chilly; awkward cupboards and passages; cellars and ice-cold sculleries; living rooms that were salons, well pickled in port and cigar smoke. Ten North Frederick. Nice houses. But the notary was old and his practice was slipping; the doctor was retired; the vet drank and his young partner did the work. The old men gathered still in the big café on the corner and played a little billiards and gossiped. It was a provincial life left over from the thirties. After the war, the burgomaster had moved to No. 1, Koninginneweg, at the extreme other end of the village that had become a town, and the Willemsdijk had slipped. Houses had passed to insurance companies, which modernized the ground floor into an office; to wholesale potato merchants and the owners of wineshops; to agencies for agricultural machinery and the County Council Road Authority.

The Koninginneweg was a poor substitute. The houses were small, mean, and gimcrack; stuccoed bungalows and little two-storied villas trying to look grand and only succeeding in looking expensive. Shoddy little balconies; ridiculous names in pastry cook's French in wrought-iron script all over the front; fake-antique carriage lamps as porch lights; unnecessary pieces of teak boarding or Tyrolean fretwork to set off the assembly-line steel windows. A lot of glass, a French window at the side, a large American auto in front for their "standing." One only has to glance at them to know what the inside is like: a wall of rough stones set in mortar, a parquet floor (coveted status symbol in Holland), central heating, and Dufy prints of yachts on the stairway. Mauve tiles in the bathroom with a matching pink washbasin and toilet.

Will Reinders lived in one of the newest, a square ugly little two-storied house standing in the few-odd square yards that is a whacking big garden in Holland, with a miniature rock garden, goldfish pond, and a plaster dwarf with a wheelbarrow. The house stood sidewise to the road, but a picture window stared out of the blank side wall. Van der Valk was standing finishing a cigarette on the pavement. He could see a youngish woman tidying the living room, and wondered how Will had organized his housekeeping. Betty had been a very house-proud woman.

He walked along a crazy pavement path and resisted the temptation to throw the cigarette end at the dwarf. Good humor was restored by a tremendous wrought-iron scrawl saying, "NOTRE SILLON."

Will himself answered the bell, a tall, thin, horse-faced man, with irregular teeth and a nose as bumpy as a country road. He was dressed to go out—camel car coat, one of those sporty ones with a violent Stuart tartan lining, a soft hat in *pied-de-poule* check, and a rather obnoxious scarf. A well-polished Opel Kapitän, self-consciously this year's model, was waiting for him.

Van der Valk gave him the business; the card that has the polite menace in it, which he barely glanced at.

"Yes?" with a slight frown. "I'm sorry but I'm due at the factory in five minutes."

"It'll get on all right without you for an hour, Mr. Reinders."

"That sounds a bit peremptory. What have I to do with—I haven't been in Amsterdam in two months."

"I will explain everything, but indoors."

"Have you the right to insist on that?"

"I'm afraid I have." Reinders checked his impatience and put on his polite face.

"Naturally, in that case, I'll help you any way I really can."

A scientific executive's living room—they tend to be dull, Van der Valk thought. An active, intelligent man, but with little feeling for his home. Who has deliberately put off having children, because they are a drag on the career, who gives too much energy and enthusiasm to his little radio sets and not enough to what happens after he gets home and puts his slippers on.

This room was that of a nice chap, with pleasant gray eyes and an alert face. But a room with not enough flavor, not enough identity. Not false, not pretentious—just slightly boring.

Modern expensive furniture, fairly well designed and very comfortable. Warm oiled wood and tobacco-brown upholstery. Greenish Turkey carpet, with brown, beige, and ivory patterning—a nice one. A very attractive floor lamp, a slim curving trunk of natural wood with four arched branches, but clashing most heartily with the table lamp, which looked like the worst sort of wedding present. An Empire reproduction: one of those slinky, vaguely Egyptian women

wrapped in tight overlapping palm leaves and clutching a torch. A plain oblong coffee table set with tes-
serae, and above it on the wall a flashing, splashing
Karel Appel in outrageous shades of scarlet. Highly
entertaining but not belonging to the arrangement opposite it: a woolly bluey-greeny Monet riverscape over
a little writing table.

The writing table was crowned with an abominable
piece of porcelain that must be a tiger—it was painted
like a tiger—but really looked more like a dachshund.

Van der Valk got the idea that Betty had read in
Marie-Claire that the really smart woman achieves a
happy blend in her home of the modern and the an-
tique.

There were plenty of books, but they had a smirk,
as though the pages had never been cut. The books of
someone who doesn't mind spending money, who
reads reviews and buys the ones that get rave notices.
He is modern and progressive, and is all for bright
biography, piquant goosed history, and new-wave fiction. He has them in the house and will get around to
reading them just as soon as he finds a minute.

Reinders jerked a hand abruptly at a chair, sat
down himself gauchely (his legs were too long), and
looked as if he were about to bite his nails. He suddenly got sick of Van der Valk's admiring his furniture.

"What am I supposed to have done?" irritably.

"You aren't supposed to have done anything. I am
inquiring into the circumstances of a series of events,
one of which is your wife's death."

"Oh, no, not again."

"I quite agree and I would have much preferred not

to bother you at all. This time it's for keeps. It has been decided, in everyone's interest, to work as far as possible incognito. Which means you may know who I am but you are one of a small select group. A happy family, like the Bluebell girls. Not even the local police know who I am; I want this to sink in. To you and everybody else I am a busybody official from some Ministry or other doing sociological reconnaissance. This conversation is in complete confidence."

"Who gets whose confidence?"

"I mean that if you tell the truth in answering possibly embarrassing questions, it doesn't have to go any further, but if you tell stories, I'll know. The franker you are, the less finagling you give me, the quicker it's all over."

"I've been frank with all the other policemen and it hasn't been the faintest help to anybody."

Van der Valk gave him his slight subtle diplomat's smile.

"I'll help you. A piece of listening apparatus, secret, very sensitive, disappeared from this house. Your boss told me that. Despite the agreement to keep an uncomfortable fact dark. You may have other little secrets—mm?"

"Well, if you know that"—a rather engaging rueful grin—"I don't suppose I have anything left to hide. Ask your questions and I'll do my best. I can't say I welcome you, but at the same time it would, I admit, be a relief to me to see this business cleared up once and for all. It was never tackled head-on. In my experience as an engineer, that is a mistake."

"We're understanding each other—I am the original Head-On King. It's paradoxical, but the only way I can beat the hush-hush that gets handed out to me is by suddenly emerging from dark corners and being abrupt."

"All right. Bang away."

"Who's doing the housekeeping for you now?"

"My sister-in-law. She's a fashion photographer, but she very kindly threw a job up to come here and help me out."

"You might even end up by marrying her," Van der Valk said with helpful kindness.

"Why?" Stiffly.

"Why not? It's perfectly possible."

"I suppose you can call it that. Remotely." He sounded uncomfortable.

"Your wife's family, then, has had no thought of blaming you for her death?"

"Certainly not," with a snap. "Why should they? Some thoroughly unpleasant person—I'm glad to see you really are determined to get whoever this is— wrote filthy letters to my wife, and she suffered a nervous collapse. If only she'd told me. I was terribly busy at the time with an extremely tricky problem. Of course they didn't blame me. Betty was always a nervous girl— Well, I won't say unbalanced, but excitable. I mean that she always tended to get over wound up about things that were really of slight importance."

"Like for instance you playing with the girls in the big naughty city?"

"I'm not hypocritical about it. I haven't any mistresses or anything. Betty wasn't small-minded."

"Her family live near here?"

"No. Groningen."

"That where she comes from originally?"

"Thereabouts."

"Your sister-in-law has to stay here, then? She can't go home every night. She sleeps in the house."

"Well, yes. Natural, uh? I mean it wouldn't be logical to do anything else."

Van der Valk enjoyed these protests; he had a lever to use on Willy, if he ever needed one.

"Sleep with her yet?"

Reinders' pale skin got red as fire; he was an easy blusher.

"Why should you think any such thing?"

"Natural, uh? I mean it wouldn't be logical to do anything else." Van der Valk couldn't quite get his tone—that real engineer's devotion to a logical consequence—but he did his best.

"Look, you're insinuating—"

"You're a nice fellow, not good-looking, but the girls find you attractive. And you find them attractive. You work hard, you're an intense, concentrated kind of person, and when you want to unwind, you like to have a woman around. You couldn't help making a pass at anyone handy if Betty wasn't there. But when she was there, you gave her plenty of activity."

Reinders squirmed.

"You may as well be frank; it isn't in the least disgraceful. To use your words once again, it's natural—logical. You've often thought up games to play with Betty—making love in queer places, having her dress up in funny clothes, having her walk about with nothing on, tumbling her on the bathroom floor—on this sofa—in the kitchen."

Poor Will, he squirmed some more, but Van der Valk had him. Reinders was one of the progressive boys, believing in honesty. He had to say yes.

"Damn it, she was my wife."

"I find it perfectly reasonable. But did it occur to you that you might have been seen on one or another occasion?"

"It has, yes."

"You get on well with your sister-in-law?"

"Look—for heaven's sake—her family's very old-fashioned and strict about that sort of thing."

"You're safe from me. But you take some awful risks. They're a very God-fearing crowd around here."

"Yes. I think they're idiots."

"You aren't religious?"

"No, I'm a humanist. Of course, I respect other people's points of view. And I don't exactly publicize my views in this locality. Betty was religious—I've never held it against her."

"Your sister-in-law moved out of the guest room into yours?"

"No. I have a daily woman who does the rough work. She sees everything. Has the tongue of a rattle-snake—I don't dare get rid of her. We're very, very careful."

"Yet the person who writes letters gets to know things."

"I've thought of that, too."

"I dare say you needn't worry over much. Your wife's suicide wasn't intended, and would have the effect of scaring our friend off your private life."

"I've thought about it," viciously. "Some bastard, jealous, wanting to sleep with her himself. I know you're right and I'm a bit too fond of girls; I blame myself, too, for not keeping more of an eye on her. One of these sanctimonious, frightened, holy characters you get around here—frustrated as hell and without the guts to kiss a typist. Huh?"

"Maybe. Leave that to me; that's my job. If I get this sorted out fairly soon, you'll be left in peace to marry your sister-in-law, without there being too much gossip locally."

"I don't care a damn about the local gossip," furiously.

"I'll leave you in peace now," Van der Valk said.

He'd given Reinders an uncomfortable quarter of an hour, Van der Valk thought, grinning, as he got into the Volkswagen. The trim, very modern white Opel flew up the road back toward the "industry terrain" like a chased cat. Mr. Reinders was in a good deal of a hurry to get back to the peaceful teasing intricacies of electronics and his recurrent temptation to pat his typist's behind.

Van der Valk sat in his little auto and stared around him. There was nothing to stop him from beginning Phase 2 right away, but it was nice out there. The sky had darkened to the bilious yellowish gray of a typical snow sky, and the snow itself was drifting peacefully earthward in huge irregular lumps. He put a hand out and caught one, the size of a marble, light and feathery as eiderdown, perfectly dry but with a slightly sticky, clinging feel like a cobweb. When he drew his hand in, it just vanished, leaving no trace of moisture. Miraculous, lovely snow, making Drente beautiful.

He looked at the trees of the Koninginneweg, studying them in their new, stylized shapes. There was an old ragged plane tree, leaning out into the road at what looked a perilous angle. No—a plane was a summer tree, and no good in Drente anyway; they belonged in a hotter, drier, dustier landscape. But that yew there, stiff and upright. Menacing, like all yews—wonderful, those bony branches under the dollops of icing sugar. And that tiny Atlantic cedar in Will's ridiculous garden—pure, delicate, superb.

He got out of the car again and went back up the path, leaving footprints that looked as immortal as though this were Grauman's Chinese Theatre. He rang the bell, and paid close attention to the thermometer hanging in the dinky little porch. Zero exactly. Neither thawing nor freezing. Point of balance.

The woman who opened the door—the woman seen through the window—was now identified as Betty's sister and a lovely, brand-new, virgin, untouched witness whom no other policemen had had their great, calloused, hairy, nicotine-stained paws on.

The type of blonde that used to be called fluffy. Not really pretty enough to be a barn burner, but pleasant. Sweet. Kind. A teeny, teeny bit silly. Betty, in photographs, had not looked fluffy, but might well have been. She had been taller, thinner, and with more bone in her face. Smile. Splendid teeth. Rather a beamy waist, but plenty of hip and bosom to make up. Solid well-shaped legs with too much foot and ankle. Simply bursting with health and energy. Eyes too tiny for a big forehead, and a huge puff of honey-blond hair. He approved of all this, secretly thinking she'd be rather a bore in bed. But that was Will's outlook, not his. He remembered as a student playing the game of sitting on opposite sides of the bus and counting the number of beddable women passed.

"Oh—did you leave something behind? You were just here with my brother-in-law, weren't you?"

"I'd like a little word with you if I may, Miss Van Eyck."

"Oh—you know my name. Uh, won't you come in out of the snow?"

"Only because it's my job. I'd better introduce myself. My name is Van der Valk and I'm an inspector of police. Don't be nervous or alarmed at that—there's nothing threatening about me. I simply want to learn a little more, if I can, about your sister."

"But surely you talked to Will just now."

"Yes, indeed. And he was most helpful. Good old Will. It would be an excellent idea to marry him when all the fuss dies down. Good chap. Coming man. Fine career ahead of him."

She had gone white.

"Did—did Will tell you that?"

"Let's say that this is a little secret of yours I hold, because you have a little secret of mine. You don't know me, you don't know who I am, and in fact I haven't been here at all. I only wish to get from you a detail or two to add to what we know about your sister. Were you friends?"

"Oh, yes, always. We went everywhere together till she married."

"What is the age difference between you?"

"Just under two years."

"Did she ever tell you any little secrets after she got married?" Another big blusher.

"I don't know what you mean."

"I mean that when you saw her, as you did fairly often——mm?"

"Well, every couple of months or so maybe, no more."

"Yes—you had a nice chat together. Just between girls, between sisters. She used to tell you all about her life."

"Not particularly," evasively. Van der Valk changed tack.

"Am I right in thinking you were both always a bit rebellious? The atmosphere at home—of course, you're fond of your home and your parents, but living there was a bit oppressive sometimes, I think."

"I suppose that's true, yes."

"And Betty married a bright young fellow. And you went away to learn fashion journalism. Was that a success? Are you good at it?"

"Not very," with an honest grin.

"Did you have a good job?"

"No, rotten."

"Were you really rather pleased to have this excuse for getting out of it?"

"Yes, to tell the truth, I was, really." She gave Van der Valk another beaming grin.

"I don't suppose the idea of fashion photographing was ever terribly well received at home, either, was it?"

He got one of her straightforward naïve looks for that—how on earth did he know so much about her? He was a policeman; he knew everything.

"You persisted even though it wasn't much of a success. But you're rather happy at the idea of Will marrying you. You and Betty used to have real heart-to-heart talks about things. You both liked a good time, and occasionally, just to show you were emancipated a bit from the strait-laced ways at home, you both enjoyed feeling a tiny bit wicked."

Very wide-eyed now. Uncanny. He wanted to laugh; they were such very easy guesses and she was regarding him as an absolute sorcerer.

"You knew about Betty's boy friend, didn't you?"

"Yes," she admitted. "But there was nothing wrong, I promise. Betty would never have really—"

"Did you know about the letters?"

"No, honest. Betty just never said a word."

He was sure she was telling the truth.

"She must have got all broody about them. If she'd only said something to someone, it would have made her feel better, I'm sure."

"I'm sure, too. She didn't, unhappily. But looking back, thinking back, did she ever say anything, now that we have afterknowledge, that sounds odd, queer, unlike her, that could point to anything to do with those letters?"

"No," earnestly. "I'm afraid I can't."

"Never mind. Thank you. I hope I'll never worry you any more and"—he shook a heavy finger at her —"no tales to anyone. Remember, you don't know who I am; you've never even seen me. That's the only way I'll ever be able to find out who wrote horrible letters to your sister. So—"

"Honest."

When he came out, the snow was denser still, the lumps thicker, more cotton-woolly than ever. Van der

Valk yielded to a childish impulse, and with his face
turned upward and his grim granite jaws wide open
he did a sort of balancing act for ten good seconds
before he succeeded in catching the especially huge
one on which he had set his sights and practically his
heart. It was like spun sugar to eat—a great anticli-
max.

Arlette, the year before, had been taken by a dreadful hankering to go to the winter sports. It had all
come to nothing; her husband had not been able to get
away, and even if he had they just didn't have enough
money. While she would have been quite happy to do it
inexpensively, he would have refused; he was like that
—if you had to count pennies while you were on a
holiday, then it wasn't a holiday.

She had made do by buying all her winter-sports
clothes, and he had not counted pennies there either,
which was the advantage in having a man like him.
He had even helped her shop—saying with guffaws,
that he was supposed to be investigating a shoplifting
epidemic—and had chosen her lovely elaborate sweat-
ers, and trousers cut by a man who knew how to stick
close to solid female contours without making them
stick out. She had expensive Austrian boots, beauti-
fully soft, and the exact parkas that would be worn
that year by Mme. Express at Mégève.

Mme. Express was at Mégève, and Arlette was at
the northern end of the Dutch-German border, without
a ski slope for many miles, but damned it, here it was
hard winter, with snow underfoot, and to do her shopping she was going to pour herself into her ski *tenue*.

She was going to make pea soup; a tricky complicated business, demanding thought. Pea soup is the joy, pride—and reward—of the Dutch winter, and she was determined to insure its being good. She flattered herself that Arlette Brechignac, from the *départment* of the Var, could make pea soup as well as anyone in Holland or out.

Even in Amsterdam it needed visits to three or four shops; here, no doubt, it would be a whole damn Polar expedition. She girded up her loins to get into her black *fuseau*.

She had learned quite soon that shops that were strict about religion—and they nearly all were—could and did discourage customers from the wrong sect, either by selling them trash or simply by pretending brazenly not to have heard of whatever was asked for. Getting edible meat from the butcher was in consequence as tricky an exercise as doing the *Times* crossword puzzle—a venerable institution that Arlette had never heard of. Finding fresh leeks—now that would indeed be a miracle, but while she had given up hope of edible loaves and fishes in Zwinderen, she still clung trustingly to the miracle of the fresh leeks.

She revolved and rejected butchers as she set out, hunting for patches to walk on where the snow would crunch. It was only fat salt port, that she needed too—the staple diet of the locals—and yet somehow it was always tough, and it never tasted the way it ought to. Homesick as she had hardly ever been, even in the first days of her marriage, she comforted herself walking along the uneven brick street, filthy with truck-churned snow and sordid yellowed ice, by saying to herself the little poem by Paul Braval about the salt pork.

"Celui qui dans les boîtes de nuit
de truffes et de poulet se gave
Ca c'est un cave!
Mais c'lui qui sur le coup de minuit
Va manger un bout de p'tit salé
Place Pigalle, à la charcuterie,
Ca, c'est un affranchi!"

In Paris—anywhere, elsewhere—of course she was a *cave*. A *cave*, in the Paris argot, is anybody stupid enough to work for his living.

But in Holland, she told herself with childish pride, to fortify herself against what she knew was hatred, envy, obstinate incomprehension—here in Holland I am *affranchi!*

A little boy of fourteen or so, outside the shop of the butcher she had picked as the least of evils, turned around to goggle at her ski *tenue* and banged her leg painfully with the decrepit back mudguard of a gigantic Dutch woman's bicycle.

"Cave!" Arlette said furiously.

5

"Wonderful livid light, all lurid and sinister. I've nothing particular to go out for again; I'm going to sit by the fire and spin."

Arlette nodded but did not answer. She picked up her husband's cigarettes and took one, snapping irritably at the lighter when it didn't work; it never did for her and he could not find out what it was she did wrong, although he was supposed to be a detective.

Her face was closed and heavy; she had given herself a pugnacious double-chinned look.

"I'm making pea soup," abruptly.

That was good news. Arlette's pea soup took two days to make, but was worth waiting for. He made a vulgar noise with his mouth; she blew smoke in a loud nervous puff.

"I'll be happy when we're at home. I'm disliking all this strongly. This mean prying, this passionate interest in the foolish street—the hatefulness of it. If I lived here, I should start becoming just like the ghastly neighbors."

"Look," he said. "This is the very first time that you've ever been involved, even remotely, in work of mine. I know it's disagreeable but quite honestly I need your help. This is so simple I can't see it. So simple nobody's been able to see it. It bores me very much. I thought I'd be interested in this social-study nonsense but really I'm not. The only thing I'm interested in here is Besançon—I'm feeling that I'm even becoming friends with him. I think that's why I can't make any headway; I'm just not able to whip up interest. Today I had a talk with the husband, Reinders—remember the first girl who killed herself, poor little bitch? He's got her sister there, and is all set to marry her when the gossip dies down. In six months he won't notice any difference between her and the first one. It's dull, it's flat, it's petty—bah, I'm just as fed up with it as you are. It's my work, alas."

She managed an unwilling grin.

"Shall we have a drink to give us courage?"

"Of course. Alcohol for the machine." She poured

two. "We're not really like the neighbors, you see. They don't drink at eleven in the morning."

They drank solemnly.

"Don't worry. We'll be home soon despite everything, and when you look at yourself you'll find you haven't changed. The first day you'll be fighting with the grocer about carrots."

The grin was getting less unwilling; he didn't know whether it was the drink or the sparkling conversation.

"The first time I made pea soup"—reminiscently—"he said you didn't put carrots in pea soup. I said of course I did, and he got indignant. He said that pea soup was a Dutch thing, by God, and he wasn't going to be told how to do it by any damned French woman." She took a big drink, obviously much cheered by the memory.

"You're probably the one who can see through this at a glance. I'll show you. Where's my notebook?"

She had to go and look at the soup first. It was moving, bubbling barely perceptibly with tiny subterranean upheavals. She gave it a stir, regarded it with approval, adjusted the asbestos mat slightly, and clanked the lid back on the pot. He knew exactly. One can hear every single damn thing in these horrible little houses. And that, he thought, is just the trouble. She sat down beside him on the ridiculous sofa that was only just wide enough for the two of them and picked up her forgotten cigarette.

"There is a correlation between all these people, which I am still trying to fix. Look, now. Here—first Betty; that's the wife of Reinders, whom I saw this morning. Here's all the facts I can get about her.

"Next, the minister's wife—pretty blank. He's packed up and gone far away; I don't blame the poor devil; the gossip about him was poisonously malicious. His wife is still sitting in one of those schizophrenic apathies. They're trying the usual things on her—electricity, insulin, and so on—but they've had no very hopeful results yet.

"Here's the second suicide—the milk-products factory manager.

"Here is an interesting one—she waited some time, then brought three letters to the police. They aren't at all sure that there weren't more they haven't been shown. However, the letters then stopped abruptly, she says. If that's true, it may be significant. She's the wife of the engineer who's building that big flat-complex—he comes from near Rotterdam. And here is our new one down the road, though I won't have the police report on that till this afternoon. What I know is just facts available to everybody; he's the local sales manager for a range of imported drinks and he comes from Amsterdam.

"Lastly—I'm not able to support this at all yet— I've put down the burgomaster."

"Burgomaster?" Arlette was taken aback.

"I have a little man who is telling my stomach all the time that everything is not as it should be with the burgomaster's wife. I have to go there to pick up that report this afternoon, and I intend to try a trick on her. If it doesn't come off, I think that I could manage to smooth it all over with oily talk."

"But what have they in common with the other couples—you're talking about some correlation?"

He tried to explain. Even to him it sounded very silly.

"To start with, there's no proof that any of the allegations made in any of the letters are true at all. They all could be true, but I'm damn sure myself that most aren't true. If not all. I just don't believe that these people are the sinks of iniquity that is suggested."

"But if they aren't," said Arlette reasonably, "why on earth pretend they are?"

"That is what's eating me, exactly. The supposition is and always has been that the author spied on people, possibly with glasses, possibly listening with this tiny radio there's been a ballyhoo about, and caught people out in acts of immorality. Conclusion, the attack is on immorality. Well, I've been wondering whether there really is all that much immorality. I can't, strictly speaking, find a trace of any."

"But if there isn't, what is the attack on?"

"I just don't know," Van der Valk admitted helplessly. "The only thing I have to go on is that all the men are in positions of some influence, possibly even authority. A minister, two factory managers, a builder, a sales manager, even a burgomaster. And all of them are from outside—what we would call foreigners. Whereas all the wives are local women; that much is fairly clear. Where do I go from there?"

"You mean you want me to have a guess?"

"Just look at my notes and tell me if anything strikes you."

"Mm," dubiously. "You know me—not very bright. Still, I'll try." She read his notes carefully. He poured a second drink for both of them and looked at his wife with affection. Very nice. Her hair needed washing, slightly.

"There's a lot about religion in your notes. All these women are big churchgoers and the men aren't. Still, there's the minister, and the milk-factory man's a churchwarden. Can't be an attack on religion."

"More a defense of religion, I've thought."

"Attack on false gods? I can see that the letters are very Calvinist. But the minister . . ."

"Seems he was a left-wing minister—unorthodox, even dangerously liberal, some people thought. Miss Burger tells me that when the rumors started a lot of people were rather jubilant."

"So that a really hell-fire right-wing Calvinist would have attacked him."

"Possibly. But it's very unsatisfactory," gloomily.

"There's a feminist side, isn't there?"

"Which interests me greatly, but I can't see the point."

"The letters are somehow sympathetic to the women and anti all men. And the men are strangers, whereas the women are local. Huh?"

"It's too consistent, I think, to be pure coincidence."

"And now you feel this about the burgomaster. . . . Could it be a local reaction—I get this sort of thing each day in the shops—less against authority than—than—government interference? Industrialization? I mean that would account for Reinders, and the builder, and the sales manager, and even the milk factory—and the burgomaster could be held responsible for a lot of it, too? Anything in that?"

He sat up. "What is it exactly that you get every day in the shops?"

"Well, one feels a strong hostility to the outsiders. They call them—or us, if you like—'the import.' But there's more. There's a hatred almost of all this progress. You hear all the old wives complaining. They don't like the modernity, the progress, the new shops, or the flats really. But I don't understand it—the depression here must have been cruel. They were all as poor as rats and now they've plenty. They all have good jobs, no unemployment. How can they have nostalgia for the good old days?"

He started to interrupt but she wasn't finished.

"Of course, they all say that this building doesn't help them a bit. They moan that the new houses are far too dear for them and that nobody profits from the factories and the building but 'the import,' and that it hasn't helped them a bit. They say that despite all the new building the housing shortage is as bad as ever it's been. Even worse. Am I talking very stupidly?"

"Quite the contrary. A resentment of the outsider, plus strong conservative Calvinist religion, plus distrust of government, plus an insinuation that all this attacks morality—it could link up."

"Now I'm not following."

"You could say they dislike progress because it attacks religion, basic political beliefs, the whole foundation of their ethics. The government is too Catholic for their taste."

"You're losing me altogether now."

"The big political party here—it's called Anti-Revolutionary. Very odd-sounding to us today, but in the nineteenth century there was great strength behind it, and here there still is. Anti-liberal, anti-Catholic. The Papists are the Scarlet Woman, the schools spread false doctrine—they were opposed to all the principles of the Revolution. To them universal education and giving Catholics the vote was disastrous—practically the Four Horsemen of the Apocalypse. Now, a liberal minister would be seen as attacking them in the very sanctuary, and even the burgomaster, who is Anti-Rev himself, as well as orthodox Protestant, could be seen as the willing tool of the wicked politicians. Perhaps they all see this modernization as a corruption and a victory for the Great Beast of Rome."

"You're exaggerating."

"I've no idea whether I am or not."

Arlette heaved a deep sigh and went over to the gramophone.

"Back to the eighteenth century," she muttered, getting out her album of *Figaro*."This is too complicated for me."

"They think the same, maybe," Van der Valk said, lighting a cigar. "Before the Revolution and those horrible Frenchmen, life was much more their cup of tea."

"What, aristocratic government?"

"Why not? Man knew his place in the world. Man and God worked together for salvation, and each man could attain grace through struggle. Whereas with the Revolution, they lost their grip on God, and that worried them all dreadfully." He relapsed into scribbling; Arlette heaved another deep sigh and started on the vegetables for her soup.

6

Between Act I and Act II, they had dinner—Hamburg steak, not really very eighteenth-century, but nice. He fell into a sort of trance while Arlette did the dishes. Halfway through Act II—all the tremendous goings-on in Countess Almaviva's bedroom—he found himself just staring at the curtain of sound.

"I'm falling too deep into my theories," he said at the end of the record. "I'm going over to pick up that report—anyway, that is my pretext. I don't think the report will tell me anything much, but I want a go at Mme. Burgomaster. I probably won't be more than an hour or so."

The maid opened the door; he put on the friendly open smile of men with genuine Persian rugs to sell, made just last week in Peoria.

"Van der Valk is my name. Ask Madame to be so good as to spare me a moment."

"Oh, I have a package she told me to give you if you came—I think she's busy."

"Ask her just the same."

The girl went off obediently, but was back directly.

"I'm afraid she can't spare the time," in a saucy tone. He beamed at her—he had already marched in three steps.

"Ah. Luckily, I have plenty of time. I'll just wait till she's less busy—nice and warm in here." She wouldn't keep me waiting, he thought. She must know —or at least have a strong notion who he was. However good his alias, however cautious his behavior had hitherto been, he couldn't nose around indefinitely without being rumbled. Not in private houses.

Still, he thought, it was time to come out of the shell a bit. As he had told the burgomaster, he couldn't just sit observing for an eternity. Neither the taxpayer nor the Procureur-Général would stand for that. Time for Van der Valk to show a little action.

Sure enough, there she came, rather white around the nose, too. Full of indignation. Now, what had she to get indignant about?

He had a feeling that it wasn't only indignation. Fear there, too. He hadn't done anything to make her frightened.

"My husband's at his office. He gave me a report or something at lunchtime to be left in your hands if you called. I see you have it; I cannot imagine why you should think it necessary to bother me further."

She was eying the Manila envelope in his hand as though it were the famous package in fiction that is deposited in the litter basket for the blackmailer—the big wad of used tens and twenties. He put the envelope in his inner pocket—she interested him greatly.

"I think we'd better continue this conversation under four eyes." He motioned toward the living room; she followed, stickily.

He had added several good examples to his collection of living rooms since coming to Drente; he was bitten by them the way some people are bitten by stamps or butterflies. This story, like many others, was a story of living rooms, lived or unlived. This was an excellent example of genus provincial grandeur, species higher functionary.

It was a big room, L-shaped, a pleasant room, bright and sparkling. As one came in formally, from the hall, it was dead and dry as the bones of Merovingian kings. Low coffee table in front of the window, with a tall vase of desiccated pampas grass. In the place of honor on the wall, a large tinted photograph: reigning monarch and consort, much bedizened with stars on the bosom, sashes and epaulets, not a hair out of place, glazed stares, and a general look of having eaten too much Christmas pudding. On the hearth, sawed birch logs that had been carefully dusted, and on either side a neat little electric radiator. Pale pastel rugs, beige, pink, and almond green. Large sofa and armchairs upholstered in a most expensive and grandiose stuff—cut velvet, he thought; leaf green where cut and bottle green where not cut, acanthus-leaf pattern. All decorated with silvery-green satin cushions plumped out like a poulterer's turkeys. All the seams of sofas, chairs, and cushions were bound with silver cord, with flourishes and clover-leaf hitches and at the four corners of the sofa, ending in resplendent silver tassels. It must have cost the equivalent of a year of Van der Valk's income, he surmised, and he would not have dared sit in it even in the morning coat he hired for formal affairs he was obliged to attend. On the coffee table was a presentation silver tray with a cut-glass decanter and six cut-glass whatnots designed to make grocer's port taste like Cockburn '27.

He hurried past all of it holding his breath, noting in passing a glassed bookcase with chaste blue curtains, undoubtedly filled with bound company reports and the volumes of *Punch* between 1867 and 1882.

Getting around the corner revealed a pleasant surprise; here the chairs were sat in, the television set looked at. There were engravings on the wall of views of The Hague, and the burgomaster had pipes in a rack. His wife had magazines and a Japanese lacquerwork sewing table with nests of cunning little drawers. Over the arms of chairs were little bronze ashtrays on broad leather straps, more ashtrays on the table—the ones that mustn't be used, Limoges enamel—and a vase of early daffodils. There was still a strong feeling that dogs and policemen were not permitted, but it was at least human.

Van der Valk wasn't asked to sit down.

"And what, Mr. Van der Valk, can you have to say to me that is private—and what, I wonder, gives you the right to order me about in my house?"

"A burgomaster, Madame, is an important state functionary. No questionable interpretation can ever be put on his actions, or his family's; that is self-evident."

"I fail to see . . . this impertinence . . ."

"If it were ever suggested—malicious tongues are never lacking—that there were some irregularity— misuse of municipal funds, anything you like—he can —he must be able to disprove it openly and at once. Isn't it so? And of course he can; everything is on paper. His private life must also be above damaging insinuation. If anybody makes such remarks about an ordinary citizen, he can be sued for slander, but suppose a whispering campaign were started against a high functionary in public service, it would be difficult to combat. Disregard a whisper and that is seen as a tacit admission; deny it and you simply draw attention to there being, possibly, something that needs denying. A classic dilemma."

"All very interesting. I must ask you to excuse me now."

"His wife does all she can to help, of course. Superior functionaries sometimes get—one of the thorns on their rosebush—anonymous, often vulgar, generally illiterate letters. Mostly abusive complaints from some rather simple person with a fancied grievance. You, now, have probably had similar experiences."

"Oh, my God," she said.

"Luckily, there are people whose job it is to help."

He had been wondering why the woman was acting so strangely. He had even wondered for a moment whether he had accidentally stumbled on something even more interesting than another person who had had letters. She turned the tables on him rather neatly.

"Is it you who wrote?" she asked in a terrified whisper.

He was floored. He had had to pick his way, using very pompous formal phrases, ready to cover up if he saw he was going wrong. And here he had hit a bull's-eye—and been hit a smart crack in his own bull's-eye. Van der Valk bereft of speech—extremely comic, thinking himself so clever.

"You mean you don't know who I am?"

"No—I mean I've seen you, making those secretive calls on my husband."

"You thought I was squeezing money out of him?"

"I don't know what I thought."

"Didn't he tell you, then?"

"He said it was confidential."

"I am an inspector of police, trying to sort out this rather nasty little affair. It is true that my identity was kept confidential. I am supposed to be a civil servant making a survey. I have been working with your husband—that is the meaning of these private interviews that worried you. You thought I was blackmailing him."

"He's been very worried and silent."

"Ah. He's concerned about his administration, and

his town—his folk. He's done a great deal for this place, and he cannot understand why some people, apparently, should take that amiss. You've shown him the letters?"

"I threw them all down the lavatory and I've never shown them or mentioned them. I didn't know—I thought it best to behave as though I hadn't had them."

"What did they say?"

"That my husband and I were threatened with a dreadful scandal, that he would lose his position, that —this person—would help, could stop it all, if I did what he told me."

"And what was it you had to do?"

"It was never put clearly. But—uh—something immoral. I—I knew he must be not—not normal."

"You know—or don't you?—that there have been other letters?"

"Some of the suggestions—I have been at my wit's end with worry. My husband has never mentioned it, but I have heard rumors that there have been other letters of this kind. I have even heard it said that that was why Mrs. Reinders killed herself—she was supposed to have taken an accidental overdose of sleeping pills."

"You knew her?"

"Not personally. I've met her—oh, I'm terribly sorry; please do sit down—at various functions and parties. She was quite a pleasant woman, a little nervous and abrupt."

"Church functions?"

"No, I don't think so; we didn't belong to the same church."

"You're a local woman, aren't you?"

"Well, I come from Friesland—that hardly counts as local. From the north, at least. My husband comes from Utrecht."

"Why did you think I had written these letters?"

"But how did you know I had had any?"

"I didn't. I guessed something of the sort. Your behavior arrested my attention." Delightful police language. Arresting something, even if only attention. "You have to realize that I've been on the lookout for this kind of thing. I have to—you see, people have not admitted that they have had letters. You should have told the police."

"Yes. I do see," shamefaced.

"In what sort of way are the letters written?"

"Newsprint cut out and stuck on paper."

"No, I meant the kind of language, the way of speaking."

He didn't think she was acting. Her face was still very pink; her forehead puckered up with anxious concentration. She looked like a schoolgirl who has to answer a tricky question in front of the class. She had lost the glossy self-possession of the burgomaster's wife, and her countrified, innocent look was showing through.

"They sound knowing in a horrible sneaky manner, and they kind of offer to protect me, in a beastly slimy way." She had even slipped back into the schoolgirl vocabulary.

"It's a pity you haven't kept them."

"I wouldn't have such filthy things in my house."

"They're sexy, are they?"

Terrific blush. "Well, in a certain way, yes, rather."

"What way do they sound knowing?"

"Well, saying things about my husband that nobody would know—as a sort of proof that there were other things he knew."

"For instance?"

She looked mulish. She wasn't going to tell.

"Details—of a conversation—a private one, between my husband and myself."

Now, what did that mean? Was that a euphemism for some bedtime chat? Or did it mean that the listening apparatus was cropping up again? That thing was a pest; he didn't like it at all.

"Did it say, 'I am God. I see and hear everything'? Words to that effect?" He was especially fond of the phrase "words to that effect." Never did so short a phrase contain so much.

"Yes."

"I'll have to decide what I can do. I can protect both you and your husband, so don't worry. Do nothing. But keep any letters you may get in the future. Don't tell your husband; I don't see any need to worry him. I'm here twice a week to keep him informed on my researches, so you can always get hold of me."

"I see now." Her face had lightened up, as though she were to be allowed to go to the circus after all. "I thought you were somebody horrible."

He gave his reassuring laugh: Dr. Boomph tactfully telling the wine merchant that he hasn't yet got cirrhosis of the liver.

"Be reassured. This business will soon be sorted out."

7

Van der Valk drove out along the Koninginneweg toward a less upper-crust side street leading back toward the main street. The houses were more scattered,
and there were patches of waste ground. It was freezing now; the snow on the ground had been flattened
into icy spots here and there, and he progressed with
majestic leisure, gazing around at a Drents landscape
made beautiful.

Suddenly, on the far side of the road, he saw a familiar figure that turned away from a high rusty iron
gate between two stone pillars. Besançon, in his long
overcoat, with its old-fashioned look, and rubber over-
shoes. He hadn't seen Van der Valk; he was walking
away slowly, upright, firm, but using a rubber-tipped
stick. A casual passerby would not notice the slight
quiver of the degenerating nervous system.

Van der Valk slowed the Volkswagen and stopped.
He had not noticed the gates before. The place looked
like a disused cemetery from across the road. There
was a low wall and a belt of trees. On the gates was
some plaque or inscription. He got out and walked
across to see.

Yes, a cemetery. Old headstones among rank grass
and overgrown bushes. Pretty neglected. The gate was
locked with a chain and padlock that looked as if it
had been unopened for many years. A board inside invited interested persons to apply to the municipal
gravedigger for the key, but there didn't seem to have
been any interested persons for quite a while. A tiny
cemetery in a little sleeping neglected plot of ground

with trees all around it. Forgotten, it seemed, by everyone around except possibly Mr. Besançon.

It was like his house in the disused corner of the asylum fields. Perhaps he just liked places like that. Van der Valk sympathized; so did he.

Ah, that was it. An old Jewish cemetery. The capitals of the pillars in the gateway were inscribed with thick, deep Hebrew letters. Under them was a dedication.

"To our fellow burghers, and to all our compatriots, who disappeared, carried away into night and fog, and who never returned. 1940-45" On the other pillar, a consoling if slightly banal text from the Book of Proverbs.

There had been Jews here once. Were there any now besides Besançon? No community of them, at least. Perhaps one or two isolated ones. Van der Valk could always ask Miss Burger; it was the kind of thing she could answer right away.

Strange man. Says he detests Jews, never wants to see another Jew, but that does not stop him making little pilgrimages to this spot. He feels, perhaps, his essential Jewishness more than he will admit. One does not go through the camps without knowing how deep it goes, the Jewishness.

Doubtless, if questioned, he would say it made a pleasant walk, with his slight smile, in his deep level voice that still kept a German intonation. It was less than a mile from his home, along the only street in Zwinderen that had broad quiet pavements lined with trees; it did make a pleasant walk.

Van der Valk got back in the auto and sat meditating. The only man of any real keenness he had met or

heard of around here—was that the reason his interest
in Besançon remained so vivid? Of course, there was a
lot that was remarkable about his existence. A man
who had survived where millions were massacred. Survived for five years, and in the innermost center, what
is more, of the Thousand-Year Reich. In close com-
munion with the nervous intellectuals like Schellenburg, the scientist soldiers like Dornburger, the weird
visionaries and mad idealists like Himmler, the half-
understood, misty characters like Bormann and Müller.

He knew little enough about any of them. The innermost circle—an extraordinary mixture. A few complete gangsters—like Kaltenbrunner—and a few who
remained utterly honest, scrupulous—like Berger, the
Waffen S.S. chief. It was possible, even in that circle.
Himmler himself had been in many ways very lika-
ble; kind, generous—no more than slightly crazy, one
would have thought. What impression had it all made
on a Jew, in the middle there, being cynically manipu-
lated for who knew what obscure purposes?

Some were cold and clever, merciless executants of
the horrors conceived by their fearful master. But they
had known—they must have known—that he was no
dreadful sorcerer, but a pathetic object, mentally de-
luded and physically crippled by progressive syphilitic
paralysis. They had known, and they had stayed true
to the bitter end.

Some, anyway. Himmler one couldn't count; he was
split right down the center. Schellenburg, the Intelligence chief, had played both ends against the middle,
even idealistically. And Müller—according, anyway,
to shadowy and inconclusive witness, including Besançon's—had played a game with the Russians. Perhaps

a double game? Perhaps a triple game? Who knew?
Nobody.

A Jew hadn't lived alongside people like this without learning remarkable things.

Van der Valk thought, as he often had, about that
perplexed phrase left on the report by the State
Recherche officer: "The conviction that he possessed
some secret." Mm, the deaths of a million Jews, and
the lives of a handful of the real werewolves—there
were terrible secrets there. Did Besançon believe in
God? And in the Devil? Very likely, but hardly in the
same manner as these people here, the Calvinists, the
Anti-Revolutionaries.

This town, village—whatever you called it—was
like Besançon. There was something different and alien
overlaying centuries of history. You got throw-
backs peeping through, old beliefs and old loyalties.
Deep distrusts and inborn, ingrained fears, suspicions,
superstitions. The peasants were rather like Jews,
come to that. They asked to be left alone, allowed to
have their beliefs and practices in peace. But the government, uneasy at anything that departed from the
sacred norm, could never leave them in peace. Some
busybody bureaucrat would be forever fiddling at
them. The German bureaucrats had simply been unable to stop fiddling at Jews.

Even now there was a certain power in towns like
this one. They were strong in their faith and their fa-
naticism. In Staphorst, the stranger got his camera
broken, and the wrongdoer was judged their way, according to grim rules, and given what they found, in
the Book, to be the God-ordained punishment. Just
like in Salem, in seventeenth-century Massachusetts.

The Book said, "Thou shalt not suffer a witch to live."

Here in Zwinderen they would have liked to hang witches, too. And bundle the bureaucrats about their business. Unfortunately, it was no longer possible, in Holland, to bundle senior functionaries. Burgomasters, say, or inspectors of police.

PART FOUR

KNOWLEDGE

1

AT HOME, THE VEGETABLES were in the pea soup, and a smoked sausage, too, and the perfume was filling the house. They would be allowed to eat some tonight, but only tomorrow would it reach its real glory. Arlette said it had to stand overnight before the flavor really came out. She fished the bone out then, and the piece of pickled pork. This she cut in slices and put on pumpernickel with lots of mustard—sacred accompaniment to pea soup. It isn't just soup, it's a meal, like a bouillabaisse. Van der Valk liked a calf's foot in it—he enjoyed that sticky gelatinous feel, and a soup you could really jump up and down on—but Arlette said a beef bone gave it a better flavor.

He sniffed loudly and greedily.

"Much too early yet," she said reprovingly. She was sitting almost on top of the fire—"behind the stove," as the Dutch call it—reading *Match*. "You're not to eat biscuits, either; you'll spoil your appetite."

On such a day all Holland makes pea soup. Perhaps Besançon's housekeeper would make it for him, too, and he would sit in his little room listening to the phonograph or reading, and perhaps he would feel something of the same content Van der Valk was feeling. Besançon had had a wife—gone up the chimney, one of the very first. Did the man think often of the soup she used to make? What could it be like to have no one left? No one at all.

Van der Valk felt more bored with his problem than ever. It was so unimportant, so downright trivial. An outcrop of peasant superstition and Puritan resentment. A kind of sabotage. Whoever the person was, it was somebody pathetic and half-witted. It had caused, yes, two deaths, and even that was failing to get him excited. Neither Will Reinders nor the milkman looked very tragic to him.

However, it was important; it was his job, his duty, his dedicated work. But he had to keep reminding himself of that. He couldn't help it; he felt bored with it that evening. He had the report on the affair in the Mimosastraat in his pocket—damn it. He could read it just as well tomorrow. It was an evening on which in Amsterdam he would have taken Arlette to the cinema. But not in Zwinderen, where the local pleasure palace catered to rustic youths—science fiction and ten-year-old American musicals. Tonight there was a comedy, the English kind with eccentric dukes, farcical burglars, a chase in their beloved old-fashioned autos, and a haughty dowager who clonked insubordinate policemen with her handbag.

"What are you doing tonight?" asked Arlette lazily.

"I was just going to ask you the same."

"There's a lovely Europa Cup football. Does that appeal—or are you going out?"

He didn't feel in the mood, oddly; usually the Europa Cup filled him with passion.

"I might, if you can bear to miss me."

"I'll be so excited cheering that I can miss you with ease. Hup Racing Club. I'm going to yell 'Foul!' and 'Off Side!' with the best of them."

He searched for something crushing to say. "You don't know off side from a hole in the wall."

"The wall—lovely—where they line up like chorus girls and the other side tries to get a cunning kick in over the heads." Arlette had never seen a football match in her life and didn't know the first thing about it, but was a total addict to television games.

"Something perverted about women watching football—all those sweaty jockstraps."

She just looked disdainful.

The soup was wonderful; he had the greatest difficulty in not overeating.

2

"What it is you find of interest in a boring old man with the shakes escapes me, I confess."

"What I find of interest in the rest of Zwinderen I must confess escapes me."

He was beginning by now to feel at home a little in Besançon's house; he had found the position in which to be comfortable in the creaky cane armchair, where to find the ashtray, how to get the right amount of light. The old man was accustomed to solitude, not used to repeated visits—and none at all at night—but had seemed glad to see the Inspector.

Besançon was sitting, as always, in the upright chair behind the desk. Heaven knew what junk shop he had found it in; it was an enormous ugly Victorian thing of mahogany upholstered in black leather, but they had understood comfort in those days. One could sit bolt upright, back supported, at a proper level for writing without fatigue; Van der Valk had never found a modern chair that allowed this. Besançon's desk lamp put light on the working top, where he wanted it, but the floor lamp lit the whole room just enough, a pleasant, affectionate gleam upon the books and the face. That extremely tough face, which had survived, like the Abbé Sieyès. He had been reading when the policeman came in, one of his shabby books that gave such vitality to the room. Van der Valk looked at it.

"*Memoirs of the Baron de Marbot*—heard of it but never read it—like so many others."

"Remarkable enough; full of good stories. Perhaps the only sympathetic cavalry officer there has ever been. The Napoleonic period is extremely interesting. But I incline more and more toward the thought that the world was more interesting before the Revolution."

Besançon seemed in the mood for conversation; Van der Valk had never known him so forthcoming. He had been afraid that Besançon would shut up and refuse to talk.

"More interesting, or better?" Van der Valk quite ready to rush to the defense of the Republic.

"Better if you like. People's minds were less filled with demagogic sentiments. Kings bled their subjects white building grandiose copies of Versailles, and everybody found it quite natural—they even approved."

"And we are now grateful for Dresden and Darmstadt."

"Indeed. And even the idiotic castles built by Ludwig of Bavaria. The enlightened despot is something we need. There is nothing worse than the sentimental sobbing over the common man made fashionable in the last century. I detest the common man."

Van der Valk was greatly astonished. Still, he had to keep his end up.

"But the tyrant who all too frequently takes the place of your enlightened despot can only be overthrown by revolution—by your despised common man."

"An aristocratic conspiracy," said Besançon calmly, "was cheaper, easier, and did less damage. Aristocrats might feel their privileges threatened by an abuse of power, but they protected the principle of monarchy, because in doing so they protected themselves."

"One cannot reverse history."

"Recent history is very dull. Recent history will only become interesting in another hundred years."

"When Hitler and Stalin are no longer emotional figures?"

"And when democracy, perhaps, is out of date."

"I was thinking today, oddly, in connection with my work here, that perhaps the local people would agree with you. They have a strong conservative sentiment, opposed to nineteenth-century liberalism. Probably based on Puritan religion, which wasn't opposed to monarchy at all."

"Perhaps that is why I find this countryside sympathetic. The people here may be superstitious, but they are more tolerant of an elderly eccentric than your precious government. Which cannot tolerate anything but the proclamation of the universal godhead of their infernal common man."

"You're a reactionary," Van der Valk said, grinning. "I have been thinking that my letter writer has —dimly—this sort of feeling. Someone who also detests the government, detests bureaucracy, detests the all-powerful authority of the common man. Perhaps you're right, at that. More servitude in those days, but more individual liberty, too."

Besançon gave his slow deliberate smile. "Am I being brought, after all, under suspicion of writing those letters?"

"I'm only asking whether you'd agree that letters of this sort might be a protest against the sort of society that's taking shape here."

"I have no idea. I might agree that in a bureaucratic society the bureaucrat is himself a prisoner of the system and might himself grow to resent it."

Every conversation, to a policeman, is something of an interrogation, Van der Valk was thinking. Mr. Bloodhound, with an enormous red nose, tracking clues. The drift of what Besançon was saying was interesting to Van der Valk because he had been picking vaguely at the same sort of idea. Besançon's last phrase brought him up with a start. He remembered reflecting that afternoon that Besançon's thoughts and mind must have been changed a good deal by his experiences in Germany.

"We've been talking about governments," Van der Valk said. "For a few years you lived very close to the men at the center of an important government. Did that confirm your ideas on these subjects, or have you only arrived at them by reading eighteenth-century memoirs?"

His host shrugged indifferently. "Are you interested in the Third Reich? I am not a political philosopher. What value has an idly held theory of mine?"

"I'm still interested in your ideas about bureaucracy. Remember that as a policeman I am myself the prisoner you mention."

"The Hitler regime might provide illustrations for what I have said. I saw something, certainly, of many of those men."

"Then let's hear."

Besançon looked at Van der Valk curiously, keeping silent for some time, thinking it over. He seemed to make up his mind.

"If it amuses you. I dislike talking about these episodes in my life, which have no true importance. But there can be no real objection now. It is history; they are all gone and finished.

"Where can I begin? Perhaps with the axiom that absolute power is supposed to corrupt absolutely. It is half true, like most proverbs. I said, I think, that I approve of aristocratic governments; perhaps I should have said that power is safest in the hands of those born to power, to rule, who have no axes to grind, no little revenges to take upon society. The Reich contained many cloudy idealists—Himmler, for instance —and many men with great force of character and in-

telligence, who behaved with a savagery, a vengeful-
ness, pointing to very personal reasons for behaving
as they did. Witness Heydrich, or Göring. Himmler,
you know—extraordinary mixture of imbecility and
great acumen—detested Göring and valued Heydrich
only as a highly gifted administrator. He wished to
provide Germany with an aristocracy. That was his
great aim; his S.S. was to produce this. I can quite
see his point. He became fatally entangled, of course.
What chance had he, not only against bloodthirsty
despots, but against the civil servants that made up
the third governmental group? Who possessed power
as well. Too much. Far too much."

Van der Valk listened with his mouth open. Who
would have believed that the old man would grow so
warm?

"A bureaucrat is nothing; he serves. Enclosed in a
deadening mold of formality. Unless"—slowly—"one
of them is sufficiently gifted to break out—and re-
ceives unusual opportunities of exercising great
power. Then, perhaps, he is more dangerous than the
other two kinds. For the civil servant, it is dangerous
to do anything but serve. Nothing is so dangerous as
the bureaucrat in revolt." He broke off abruptly. "I
prefer not to discuss the subject further."

"I saw you this afternoon, while I was passing on
an errand, by the Jewish cemetery. I looked at it later
with some interest; I hadn't known there was one
here."

"Jews are everywhere. These are dead ones—to
me, at least, preferable to the live ones, with their Zi-
onism—another lot busy building a bureaucracy with
their mouths."

The expression amused Van der Valk. "I enjoy hearing you on the subject of Jews."

"It is no longer fashionable to say so." Besançon's voice had lost the heat with which he had spoken of the ogres of the Reich, and had its usual tone again, detached, ironic, controlled. "But there was some truth in the accusations made against them. Aristocratic governments in earlier centuries no doubt carried in themselves their own destruction, but they were largely corrupted, rotted, by crowds of ghetto pawn-brokers. No wonder, then, that the Teutonic Knights dreamed of by that ass Himmler feared and detested Jews. A better reason than Heydrich had—did you know that Heydrich himself had Jewish blood? It was alluded to quite freely after his death."

He always says "Jews," Van der Valk thought. Isn't that unusual? Even an atheist Jew, I should have thought, says "us."

"You don't care for Jews, yet you make a little pilgrimage to their graves."

Besançon did not make the sort of excuse the policeman had anticipated.

"It was a crime, though, to murder Jews—was it not?" he inquired mildly.

3

"We won," said Arlette proudly when Van der Valk got home, not very late. "We scored three goals. They would have drawn, but we saved a penalty."

"Uh," he said, totally uninterested. He kissed her absentmindedly, and did a double take, coming back to sniff.

"You stink of drink."

"Just getting into training"—comfortably—"waiting for you to get back."

"So I see—smell, rather."

"You've had nothing?" Innocently.

"Two cups of tea. I've been with old Besançon."

"Fancy that. I thought you were bored and had gone off to pick up a Drents dancing girl."

"I do believe you're drunk."

"If that were so"—with dignity—"then I'm about to get drunker." Like a child doing a conjuring trick, she produced a bottle. "I had this hidden at home, and brought it thinking a day would come, and this is it."

He agreed that the day had come, and picked up the corkscrew. "Paul Olive," the label said. "Négociant à Frontignan (Herault)." It was yellowish, with an enormous scent that filled the whole room. He thought with some pleasure that it would not be difficult to catch up, and happily forgot all about Jews.

"I wish," she was saying dreamily, half an hour later, "that I had a garter belt with little silver bells on."

It wasn't till he was half asleep that he remembered he still hadn't read the report about the couple down the road, and he snickered. Arlette had her ways of combating her dislike of being a suburban housewife in an identical row of tiny mean houses in the Mimosastraat. How many of the housewives of Zwinderen, he wondered, danced tangos in their living rooms dressed in a garter belt? His snicker must have been sensible, if not audible, because Arlette muttered sleepily, "Shut up. In my present condition I mustn't be vibrated."

4

It was the most unpleasant sort of Dutch weather the next morning. By the thermometer not so very cold—six below zero—but not a hard, clear, bearable cold. A thick sullen mist hung on the sour landscape, and a small mean wind pierced everything but a leather coat. Never had the little living room, with its dreary furniture belonging to nobody, seemed so uncomfortable. Van der Valk settled down with his report and his notebook, annoyed with himself for not being able to take it all more seriously. Perhaps it came from not having an office to go to; he was a creature of routine.

When these affairs aren't cleared up in a day, they always tend to take three weeks, he told himself. In the next breath he was telling himself that he ought to have been on top of it by now. He would be getting a reprimand for wasting public funds.

Working in this left-handed way, snooping in a pretentious shroud of anonymity, which everybody had probably seen through by now. What was he doing away from paper work, from the familiar police smell of the room in the big building on the Marnixstraat, from the old-maidish fussing of Mr. Tak?

What was he doing away from his home?

He had to make an effort. Look, three-quarters of Holland lives in the Mimosastraat, in one or another provincial town, and provincial towns are the same all

over Europe. Think of one of the really dreadful
French towns. Meanness, nosiness, obstructionist petti-
ness—every bit as bad as here and probably worse.

Still, there he wouldn't find the sixteen different
churches. Bigotry, yes; sex, yes; and a prudish love of
secretly using four-letter words—but this Calvinism?

Or the ghastly heath country south of Hamburg—
they had witches there. There was a doctor in Hamburg who was an expert on witches.

Sweden—this cocktail of provincial sex and Calvinist religion was common coin there, to go by what
one heard.

He wished he knew more, that he was not so ig-
norant, so inexperienced, so damned helpless. There
was nothing extraordinary about this. This little town
in Drente wasn't unique.

The report was no great help. The couple down the
road had committed no offense, not even a misdemeanor. The struggle to stop the car—driving without
due care and attention, twenty-gulden fine. It was the
fear of publicity more than the twenty gulden that had
helped the police twist these people's arm a little.

There had been letters, all right—claimed destroyed. Frustrated again; he wished he could get his
hands on one letter, just one. The usual stuff, it
seemed. The husband had been accused of corrupting
the morals of all and sundry, peddling the demon drink
of course, and being free with waitresses. The wife
had taken it seriously, because there was some truth
in it, apparently, and she was a jealous woman. She
had made a scene. The man had wanted to go straight
to the police, and this had upset her even more. To
have the police in the house—well, now she had

them. The husband had turned on her defensively and accused her of carrying on with men herself. She had boiled over then into a galloping hysteria. Anonymous letters—they should be me, Van der Valk thought. I've had dozens; one always gets a few if one's name is in the paper during an inquiry.

No, it was not conclusive; just one more straw. There was perhaps a grain of truth in the allegations —the husband was one of those self-satisfied men, conscious of having good looks and a glib tongue— but our letter writer never seemed to care greatly whether an accusation was true or not. Perhaps they were true in his mind. But whether true or false these letters could be very effective—upon the right character.

The engineer from Rotterdam—his wife had given the letters to the police, too. He didn't care about them and neither did she. On inquiry, he seemed to be vaguely but generally known as a skirt chaser, and she as respectable as all the other wives. Using his alias, Van der Valk had got Miss Burger to turn up some papers relative to the flat-complex, had questioned her idly, and had heard a bit of gossip. Not that the woman was a gossip in the neighborhood sense—Mrs. Tattle over the garden wall—she simply knew everybody. One does, as the burgomaster's secretary in a small provincial town.

He was still floundering. What was the significance of the listening apparatus? It had disappeared all right. He had never believed that it had played any real part, though. He had said, of course, that otherwise things were unexplainable, but that had been to twist what's-his-name's arm, the owner of the factory.

He hadn't believed it. All the knowledge shown by the writer was either vague gossip—surely known indirectly to any number of people—or quite likely invented; it couldn't be proved either true or untrue.

The only piece of evidence that sounded conclusive on that point was the remark made by the burgomaster's wife, that the letter writer had shown knowledge of a private conversation. Hm. He had been told in Amsterdam to be very discreet indeed. He had better go easy with the burgomaster.

Why was it that whenever the police had started inquiring, letters had ceased, information had dried up, nothing had got anywhere? It was as though the letter writer had some mysterious knowledge of the police activities, and in detail, too.

Van der Valk had thought of that a long while ago, and had made a list of the people who had known something of what was going on and what the police were up to during the long series of dragging inquiries. He had thought that line of investigation might possibly get him somewhere. But it had petered out, too.

The burgomaster himself, of course. His locum, the senior town councilor. The chief of the local police. The secretary to the town council. Miss Burger—not officially, but it was plain that she was in the know about everything. Not a very encouraging list. He had done his best with it for days, ever since he had come here, in fact. Five civil servants, all efficient, all blameless, all involved in church activities and social works. Organizers of charities. All married, solidly, worthily, all with children of school age—except Burger, of course, who lived alone in a flat. Equally blameless—he had observed from a discreet distance;

he had even rummaged a bit about the building and the inhabitants of the block. The flats were in a double row of three to the block, six to a common entrance, and in a block like that not many of the movements of any one are missed by the other five. Miss Burger was a devout churchgoer, a pillar of the Rural Christian Women's League, the Consumer's Bond, and the Association for Better Housing.

The locum-burgomaster was keen on scouting and sport. Energetic about gymnastics for school children, about jamborees and educative trips abroad to ancient Greece and such. If there were any mountains in Holland, he would have climbed all of them. He was the moving spirit behind the local volley-ball team and the projected skating rink, and had been the promoter of the rather grand swimming bath. His wife was a good soul, a model housewife and mother, whose children were impeccably sent every two weeks to get their hair cut. Man and wife were both given to the activities of the Good Neighbors' Association, where twice a week they solemnly played bridge or listened to little lectures.

As for the municipal secretary, he was the heart and soul of the Operetta Club. Besides being quite a good violinist, he played checkers.

All these people were Reformed and Anti-Revolutionary. Damn it, Van der Valk thought, what can I do with people like that? Rotarians, Pickerbaughs. Philistines, yes, tedious Do-Gooders, whom personally he found unsympathetic but public-spirited, with social consciences, backbone of civic virtue.

He thought again about the striking remark Besançon had made the night before. That if a bureaucrat

once moved into rebellion he would be a most dangerous person. It might be true. Probably in the Reich it
had been true. This, however, wasn't the Reich. This
was Holland.

Odd how all roads led back to Besançon.

Van der Valk was slipping into a lard-like weari-
ness and discouragement. He wasn't a step further.
And yet he was so near. Why, he wondered, don't I
get a tiny stroke of luck? He polar-beared up and
down the box of the room. There was still something
he had not seen, was too stupid to understand.

He wanted to walk, but the weather was vile. The
car was in the garage with some obscure ailment and
would not be ready before evening. He didn't want a
drink. Since coming to Drente, he had drunk double
what he did at home. There he would have an *apéritif*
if he happened to be at home—and if he happened
to have the time once he did get home. The occasional
bottle at night split with Arlette. On weekends, perhaps a cognac after dinner. Whereas here he was
drinking two or three drinks at all hours. I'll have to
stop that, he thought. Getting a bit tipsy to encourage
Arlette to get tipsy, sexy, and thoroughly enjoy herself was one thing. Being on the way to becoming a
sort of small-time bedroom drunk was quite another.

He put his coat on, muttering, and stamped out irritably. It was every bit as disagreeable out as he had
been led to believe. On the way he met Arlette, cross,
coming back from shopping. Usually he fetched her
heavy shopping with the car; now, of course, the nas-
tiest day of the year was the one on which he had no
car.

Unhelpful situation. On the one hand, whole rows

of worthy citizens possessing the information needed to write those letters. He couldn't quite see them possessing the necessary malicious imagination, let alone creeping about peering, listening.

On the other hand, Besançon, capable of imagination, of unexpected ideas or, very likely, actions. But even with twenty telephones and a portable X-ray how could he have known enough about all those people to write those things? If there had been invention, it was cunningly interwoven with fact.

It was ridiculous, he thought, to start suspecting Besançon of anything now. All the others had suspected him, so he deliberately hadn't, out of vanity. But what was it about the old gentleman that so drew the policeman's eye? He had told himself that his eye was drawn by anyone interesting and intelligent—that was complete nonsense. The more one sees of him, he thought, the more one feels that there are questions there that need answering. A sulphurous smell, a sort of mephitic air.

The State Recherche officer, a special-duty man from the political police, accustomed to aliens and refugees, everything and anything peculiar, had been baffled. Had been driven to the unsatisfied, unhappy, helpless annotation on his report that had fascinated Van der Valk right from the outset. With the best will in the world he could not see the old gentleman writing dotty letters.

What old gentleman? He was not far into his sixties. Still, his hardships, his past, his illness had put ten or fifteen years on him.

The inspector from Assen had conducted a little experiment. He had asked Besançon, politely, to cut a

178 DOUBLE BARREL

page of newsprint into little squares like those used for the letters. With a pair of nail scissors, which the experts declared to be the instrument used. He had obeyed calmly, not asking questions, though he said he had no idea what it was all about. Despite his shaky hands, his morsels of paper had been neatly snipped, but though they looked good enough, the microscope showed up a characteristic unevenness, in keeping with his disease, that the original letters had not had. Analysis of these could be brought no further than to a guarded hypothesis that the snipper had an orderly mind and meticulous habits. Characteristics, Van der Valk thought crossly, that Besançon shares with two-thirds of Holland. The paper the letters were pasted to came from the Hema, the Dutch Woolworth's, as did the paste; every family in Holland possesses a pot.

The fresh air was beginning to wake him up; he strode along like a town-scoutmaster on his way to some damned hillside where he could fill his lungs with the damned healthy fresh air. But he still felt like Mr. Verloc, who, Conrad said, had the air of having wallowed all day, fully dressed, upon a disordered bed. Van der Verloc.

The gardens of all the little houses, so trim and neat in summer, were untidy with frostbitten leaves and messy stalks left over from autumn, with drifts and patches of frozen snow. All the housewives had religiously swept their paths and patches of pavement, and the dirty, trampled snow was piled messily in the gutters, but on the minute lawns it still lay virginally. Underneath, Van der Valk thought, there are tiny green shoots—snowdrops, crocuses. It is nearly the end of February after all, he thought; spring is on its way to Drente. The clematis and jasmine on the outside walls will be waking up; the stiff pointed buds of the rhododendrons swelling. Soon a faint tinge of green around the lilac twigs. Sap and life stirring everywhere in the barren-looking sour ground.

"Except in my stupid head," he muttered loudly. Two teenage girls, clinging to the same bicycle, turned their untidy scarved heads, stared, and giggled in unison.

5

He plodded obstinately on, the whole length of the village, all the way to the "industry terrain." He wanted to see Reinders. He thought it might have been a mistake to have talked to Will at home.

Generally it was a good idea. It seemed obvious to him that if you talked to somebody—pretty nearly anybody—in his own living room, you stood a better chance of penetrating the things that are nearly always there to puzzle one. There are flaws in all this, of course, perhaps the biggest being that there aren't any simple explanations to anything. Often there just aren't any explanations. Another big flaw is that there are lots of people who aren't at their most natural or even at their most confident in their own living rooms.

Willy, now—at home had he felt himself hampered, uneasy? Yes, and not only on account of the girl there, her physical presence, dusting in the next room. And not only on account of things Betty had bought and chosen, herself handled, polished, dusted. It was still Betty's house, but there was even more than that. Will had been defensive and Van der Valk had been clumsy. He had struck false notes, and Will had been soured as well as harried. He had to try to do a bit better.

The timekeeper at the barrier recognized Van der Valk, told him in a gleeful way that the boss wasn't there today. Van der Valk looked pained and pensive.

"Now, who had I better see?"

"Well, there's Mr. Smit—he's the Production Manager."

"No, Mr. Reinders, I think; I've had the pleasure of meeting him already." He sounded fussily self-important; he was good at this role of the Man from the Ministry.

"I'll phone him for you."

He could hear Will himself on the wire; he had a vibrating, emphatic voice, and sounded jovial.

"What gentleman? Oh, Mr. Van der Valk; yes, I know. Yes, by all means. Can he find his way, or shall I send a girl?"

"I'll find it," Van der Valk said. There was a rigmarole of staircases and passages, but he was, after all, a detective, which was helpful when it came to finding Room 9.

Nine was a sort of drawing office, not much different from an architect's, with those angled boards and the lamps and rulers that have shoulder joints and elbow and wrist and finger joints, and make it all look so easy. Two effaced pipe smokers were busy making dodecaphonic electronic musical notation. Van der Valk hurried on, scared, into an office with a cross-eyed girl typist and a bustling middle-aged efficient female who told him she was the Assistant to the Director. She was cheery but not very pinchable.

At last he got to Willy, right on the inside—a big office with a large metal desk, very untidy. There was a wall of bookshelves full of the kind of stuff Mr. Besançon got asked to translate. There was a round table with a large model airplane standing on it, a sofa against the wall with a coffee table in front, and the fourth wall was window, with climbing plants and a view of the Drents hinterland. By his desk Will didn't have charts with statistics, but a blackboard with more electronic music scribbled on it. This was freehand, without benefit of mechanical elbows, and the result reminded one of the maze puzzles in children's magazines. How will Bobby Bear get out of the witches' forest? (Remember, there is only ONE way he can be safe.) Van der Valk took a look and decided that Bobby Bear had taken the first to the right three times too often already and was about to be bagged by an ogre.

Will was wearing a loud tweed jacket, had glasses on, ink on his fingers, and chalk on his sleeve. He would have looked like the mathematics master at the local grammar school but for a dead filter-tip cigarette he was chewing on. He followed Van der Valk's look.

"People enjoy reading music, I'm told—if they can read it well enough. This isn't any different."

"And the airplane?"

"Oh, that. I built it. We've used it for various experiments—teleguiding, and so on."

"Clay pigeon."

"Exactly." He seemed pleased. "Sit down if you

want." The Inspector sat on the arm of the sofa. Will leaned his backside against the desk and just looked amiable and not a bit worried.

"You do computers and things here?" Now Will looked amused, too.

"Good God, no. That's something you leave to the big boys. Only Bull does that, here in Europe, and even they look like getting swallowed by the Americans. I once built an electronic cooking stove but my wive didn't like it. Preferred old-fashioned heat. Scared her—too uncanny." He grinned, and then stopped grinning. "I'm glad you came. I couldn't talk about it at home. Not with Cat there. It must have looked to you as though I hadn't cared for Bet at all. And I did, you know."

He was getting younger every minute. He was looking about nineteen now.

"She wasn't unhappy. She liked it here, even. It meant a lot to her that I got this job. She got a fine new house; she was proud I had a job I enjoyed and was good at." He stared at his blackboard. "I know of course it wasn't enough. This is a hell of a competitive world. But how would I have guessed it would go so far? Where did the catastrophe begin?"

Van der Valk said nothing. Did Will think he knew, or something?

"You know, electronics is not a simple thing either. If these toys were that simple, everyone could have teleguided missiles. You wish, let's say, to provide certain impulses, make an inanimate object obey various complicated rules. You cook up a system of circuits and on the board it looks foolproof. You put it together and build it into your machine on the test-bed; it works perfectly. You repeat it exactly in practice, and for no reason at all that anyone can understand it goes haywire, just does illogical things. You may very well never find out why, even after months of patiently studying and checking and recalculating. It seems good, but it just doesn't work. The only thing is to just scrap it, forget the whole thing, start building again from scratch. You haven't even gained any real experience to profit from, to tell you what to avoid."

He was looking at Van der Valk now with open appeal.

"I did my best. I thought she had a good life. I didn't neglect her, really. I mean I thought about it; I thought she was occupied and contented and not sexually unsatisfied or anything. I suppose I just committed the mistake of thinking people are fairly simple, compared to electronic circuits."

"A neurologist told me once," Van der Valk said vaguely, "that the human body makes electronics look in comparison like the first steam engine." Will suddenly found the dead butt in his mouth and tossed it angrily into the big gray metal wastebasket.

"I wouldn't know. We're told that if something goes wrong it's human error—must be human error—but you feel often enough that nothing you do makes any difference." He sat down abruptly at his desk.

"I'm talking too much. Did you want to ask me something—or tell me something?" He lit a fresh cigarette, realized he hadn't offered his caller one, and held the packet out with an apologetic "Sorry."

"No. I just wanted to see this place." He seemed pleased.

"But I couldn't explain, not in years."

"I can't explain anything either. There isn't any explanation."

"For Betty? But I blame myself."

"So do I."

He looked mystified, but didn't press it.

"Can't blame everything on the pilot's error," Van der Valk told him. "If the little black box doesn't function—"

"One of these days," Will said heavily, "the little black box won't function, and their old bomb will poop off where they least expect it. Then we're all in the soup."

Van der Valk laughed at him then. "You'd better start believing in God," he told him, mischievously.

"I wish I did sometimes. Would you like some coffee? I haven't anything much to do this morning, to be honest."

"Sure." Despite Van der Valk's confiding character, he didn't tell him he hadn't anything to do, either.

Van der Valk lit a cigarette, too, to be friendly. Of course Will wasn't responsible for her death. And of course he was, as well. But that wasn't any of Van der Valk's business. All the fault of the little black box.

Van der Valk walked on. Perhaps semiconsciously he turned into the Koninginneweg. Here the housewives did not do menial chores like sweeping pavements, and the daily girls dodged it—it wasn't their pavement; his footsteps were muffled, and creaked sometimes on snow still untrodden. He had no idea at all what to do. He passed Will Reinders' square ugly little house and thought it had the same awkward innocence as the giggling girls on the bike. He did not think there was any crime there. He reached the big house on the corner—a grand affair for this five-cent town, flashing with polished brass and fresh paint. He didn't think there was any crime there, either. His road was leading him toward Besancon, inevitably. What could he do about it? In some way, there lay the key to what he was searching for.

The sagging little cottage behind its high wall and ragged row of cypresses was older and wiser than the houses in the Koninginneweg, he thought, looking through the chink in the gate. He hadn't any reason for doing so but he tinkled the bell. Placid Mrs. Thing came out with her duster in her hand. She showed no curiosity at seeing him—the only one in the whole of Drente that hadn't, he thought. Or perhaps Miss Burger? No, that was more professional discretion. He thought of questioning her and decided not to. Her deposition was on the file—what more could she have to tell him?

She smiled with friendly recognition.

"Will I bother him? I realize it's working hours."

"I think he'll be glad to see you. He's shaky these last few days—can't settle to his work. He's not getting any better, you know," she added rather sadly. "But there's nothing the doctors can do, they say." Van der Valk could see that she was fond of Besancon.

"Is the road really going to be widened?" she asked as she shut the gate carefully behind him. "It would be an awful pity. You can't see it at present but he's done wonders with the garden."

"I'm pleased to see you," said Besançon, getting up and holding out his hand. There was a spark of cordiality in the quiet controlled voice.

"Sit down, then, in your usual chair. Mrs. Bakhuis will bring you coffee, I feel sure; she approves of you."

He was not at all surprised that Van der Valk kept coming.

"You can't really be pleased to see me."

"Why not? You are agreeable company. What good would it do me to be displeased? I cannot stop you coming. You are a policeman, and despite a certain unwilling sympathy you have for me, you suspect me. You do not know why, but you do."

"Perfectly true—and very silly."

"You are an intelligent man, Mr. Van der Valk. Stupid people stare at me owlishly, and I know they feel resentment, perhaps hatred, at my being different from the people they are accustomed to. Whereas I see your eyes constantly on me, not rudely, but trying to understand what it is that puzzles you. Yet it is all in the dossier." He sounded resigned, as though he knew Van der Valk would never understand.

Besançon looked very small and thin in the high-backed solid chair. He rested his hands in his lap, loosely folded together. The policeman studied the thin gray hair, the lines in the face like ax cuts, the sharp flicker of the very bright eyes behind the mask of dark glasses. The mouth so tightened and pulled and reined in through long years that the lips scarcely showed. As always, he was carefully shaved and spotlessly neat, wearing his shabby well-brushed jacket as though it were a full-dress uniform with gold lace. He looks like Captain Dreyfus, Van der Valk thought, after his epaulets had been torn off in public. He has a lot of dignity. Now, there was another one to whom suspicion had clung obstinately, quite without reason. Even after the rather clumsy plot had been exposed, kind and honest people had refused to abandon their conviction that he was a villain and a traitor. And even now, Van der Valk thought, people are ready to believe Jews capable of anything, from cheating the tax inspector to ritual child murder.

Am I like that, too? he wondered. I have, after all, nothing, absolutely nothing, of which I can suspect this man.

"You do not, in the least, have a Jewish physiognomy, do you?"

"I know—or knew—Jews with blond hair and blue eyes."

"But we still go around thinking of Jews as round-shouldered, hook-nosed, with big moist cunning brown eyes and thick sensual mouths?"

Abruptly, Bensançon changed the subject. "How long have you been a policeman?"

It surprised Van der Valk, but he had a perfect right to ask. Why not?

"Since 1946. Straight out of the army. I was one of those dimwit idealists." That earned him the slight vivid smile.

"A policeman is like a doctor, I thought," Van der Valk said. "He serves society. The naïveté of both these ideas—"

"You have acquired a professionalism, a competence—and the usual police skills. But not the real police mentality."

"You understand me better than I do you."

"Yet you have had a successful career." Van der Valk looked sour.

"You have had disillusion, bitter moments?" he added.

"Certainly. But I am lucky enough to have a wife with a very strong character."

"Ah."

Van der Valk could not see enough of the expression around the eyes, behind the dark glasses.

"Tell me more about your life."

"I am one of those characters that like the wrong things and too often the wrong people. I thought myself a fair boxer when I was a boy. Thought—I was a fair boxer. I thought myself a second Cerdan. But boxing is not considered respectable here—unsuitable for a public servant. I wanted to study languages, medicine, psychology—I had ideas that those things would be a help. But I had no choice; I didn't have the money for studies, you see. I got put to studying jurisprudence—very dull. Out of sheer rage, probably, I passed my examination to become a police officer. Went to the school for cadet officers. Got top marks in my class. Found out later that I'd got the worst recommendation in the class, too, from the instructors. I became an inspector, but I've been reprimanded a dozen times, seen my seniority clipped twice for exceeding instructions. I know that my promotion is blocked. If I hadn't been lucky and occasionally solved a few little puzzles that had floored the orthodox, I'd probably be clerking behind a desk. I'm here now—it will be another question of luck. If I clear this up smartly, after a lot of others have balled it all up, it will do me a lot of good, and if I don't, as seems extremely likely, I'll be in the doghouse forever, probably."

"You lack the art of pleasing your superiors." The smile had crept back.

"I lack pretty nearly everything. And especially the right mind. A fellow who was junior to me—and even a little stupider—got made chief inspector a month ago."

Besançon leaned forward on the desk and seemed wrapped in some thought of his own. Van der Valk looked at the books. Memoirs, history, astronomy, seventeenth- and eighteenth-century writers; books in Russian, in French, in German. Suddenly Besançon said something rather astonishing.

"You will clear this up, all right. It would not surprise me if you cleared up a lot of other things, too, that have for long remained obscure." The policeman looked surprised.

Besançon got up abruptly. "I will ask you to excuse me. I do not feel well, and I think I wish to lie down for a short time."

At that moment the door opened. Mrs. Thing— Van der Valk never could remember her name—with coffee for him. Besançon smiled.

"You must not think I am chasing you away. Sit here quietly, have your coffee in peace. Here." He picked up a book from his desk and gave it to his guest. "Read that for a while, and fortify yourself." The dramatic works of Corneille. Well, Van der Valk thought, I certainly could do a great deal worse. Besançon gave him a look as he went out. "Learn what you can," it seemed to say. "Conclude what you

like." He shut the bedroom door behind him with no
further interest in what Van der Valk did.

The coffee was too hot to drink. Van der Valk
walked about, staring at the bookshelves. He sat down
aagin deliberately in Besançon's chair, at his table. He
bit into a biscuit and brushed the crumbs away. He got
up again to look at the record folders, rummaged
through the long row of cardboard files containing
typed manuscripts, and left them alone again with a
wrinkled nose. Technical German and Russian—jaw-
breaking jargon; a language of its own. His German
was none too good at the best of times.

All German music—no Frenchmen or Russians,
nothing from the romantic period. Haydn, not much
Bach, surprisingly little Beethoven. No, here was later
stuff. Gluck, Weber, *Vogelhändler, Schwarzwald-
mädel*—operetta, by heaven. And such German operetta. Opera? No Wagner, no Mozart, no Italians. But
plenty, plenty of Richard Strauss. Remarkable.

There was nothing on the desk; no memo pad, no
diary. Nothing like a photograph, a present, an orna-
ment, a souvenir anywhere in the room. The room of
a man who came back walking, wearing refugee charity clothes, carrying nothing. Everything that happened before 1945 wiped clean out. Fair enough.

On the desk was a Bible in old Gothic German,
printed in Leipzig in 1911, and two surprises—the
memoirs of Charles de Gaulle and a biography, in
English, of Oliver Cromwell. The one Van der
Valk could understand—Besançon was interested in
the problems of power—and the other? Cromwell's
sources of power? Cromwell's Calvinist conscience?

Was it not unusual that there was no book in the

whole room that had anything to do with Jews? Except Feuchtwanger's best seller of the thirties, *Jud Süss*. And that was a novel.

There was nothing there for Van der Valk or that was any of a policeman's business. He went home. There was a pork chop, cooked in the oven with an onion and an apple, sage, garlic, and bread crumbs, with mashed potatoes. Good. Endive *à la crème* to follow. And an orange.

6

He wrenched his mind away from Besançon, who was only distracting him from his business, and he went, that afternoon, for a long, long walk alone. His report to the burgomaster was due that evening. He was rather late; he had to go home and change his shoes; he had to walk to the garage to pick up the car, and they made him wait, of course. He thought, while he was walking, about the people who were so obviously out of place here, like Will Reinders. For a first-class mind, he was a singularly naïve man. He made it so difficult for himself. He had to put "Religion, Reformed," "Politics, Anti-Rev.," on all the little forms; he had to pay lip service to all the conventions he detested; and he did such silly things.

Like me, Van der Valk thought. Still, I don't have to live here.

Reinders had a better job than he would have had anywhere else. The owner had explained to Van der Valk that he kept his business in Zwinderen because his costs were two to three per cent lower than elsewhere in Holland—and it was just this money that he could devote to research, at which Reinders was a good man. Poor old Will, stuck in Drente.

It will obviously never occur to him, Van der Valk thought, that he is in several senses responsible for his wife's death—nor that to marry the sister will hardly put an end to his problem.

Van der Valk thought about the lover boy, the draftsman who had been given the sack. A juvenile Reinders—another boy who did not believe in governments or churches, who had thought it virtually a sacred duty, as well as the handiest expression of his revolt against convention, to make love to his boss's wife. Poor Betty, she had had a hard time. Van der Valk wondered whether she'd ever got as far as sleeping with the boy. Reinders would not be a difficult subject to cuckold.

Van der Valk thought about "the import," the other men and women who had the responsible jobs in the local factories, who lived on the Koninginneweg, who put up with Drente because they had good jobs, but were certainly all on the alert for better jobs that might get them out again. None of them had had letters—had they? They were the ones most likely to bring letters to the police if they did. Their positions were secure, and independent of what Zwinderen said or thought. It was only the local women—like Betty, small-town women all their lives—who cared what Zwinderen said or thought. She had tried so hard. He recalled one of Will's stories; Will had talked (and how he had talked) freely once Van der Valk got him going. Betty had been interested in a book that had caused a lot of stir, about incest or something. Will had bought it for her in Rotterdam. She had read it pretending indifference, but he had seen, he said with intolerable self-satisfaction, that she had been much shocked. Poor Betty.

Now, how to explain to the burgomaster that the nets were undoubtedly getting very narrow but that Van der Valk still had no fish? Ah, there was the car ready at last. The mechanic gave him a long lecture about the vitals of a Volkswagen, in which he wasn't the least interested.

In the burgomaster's study, papers were being sorted out, a lot of municipal bumph for the next day's council meeting. Van der Valk said his little piece; the burgomaster seemed fairly satisfied.

"Burgomaster, I have a small but pertinent question, which I must ask you not to take amiss."

"Ask, by all means."

"I'm aware, of course, that you treat municipal affairs with the utmost discretion. But I would like to know whether any unauthorized person could ever get access to any confidential memoranda."

"Oh, I understand. Similar questions were asked by the State Recherche—they were very thorough. I don't take it amiss. In this house—I often have papers here in this room. But they are kept in this cabinet, of which I have the only key. Surely there's a note to that effect in your file?"

"There is, yes. It was, paradoxically, more the complete opposite that I was thinking of. Could any personal papers of your own—perhaps a private letter, or something concerning family affairs, your wife, for instance—ever get mixed up with any official work you might have here? So that a letter, say, got brought inadvertently to the office?"

"I've never thought about it."

"Why should you? The security aspect is all on the other foot, so to speak."

"It could happen—it has no importance, though."

"Can you recall any such occasions?"

"Two or three, I think. Letters get into my brief-case—people who think that by writing a personal letter to my home they will somehow get a more favorable reaction. Begging letters, mostly. Miss Burger deals with them. Occasionally a genuine personal letter has got mixed up with those, probably because it had a typewritten envelope or some such reason."

"Has anything of the sort ever happened that bothered you—I mean some item of news or information that was really no concern of anyone bar you? Of course, I realize that it would only reach Miss Burger and go no further."

"On that account I would have no worry—she's discretion itself. I do recall once a letter that I'd picked up on my way to work and had stuffed in my pocket. It came inadvertently under her eye and caused me, I admit, some slight embarrassment. But as soon as she read the first lines and realized its personal import, she handed it straight back to me, apologizing profusely."

"Have you any objection to telling me what was in it?"

"You're not suspecting Miss Burger, are you?"

"No, no, just a cross-check."

"Well," he hemmed, "it was a letter from a doctor —a medical matter—concerning only myself. I'm afraid that's all I can tell you."

"No matter."

"If you're concerned whether Miss Burger could

have discovered your identity. I can reassure you. I have a 'For my eyes only' file—the correspondence relative to your purpose here went in that."

"That does indeed reassure me."

"Oh, I dare say Miss Burger has a certain curiosity about your doings. But she's not only well trained— she has a very strongly developed conscience."

"Conscience as a worker?"

"Not only conscientious—that's not so rare, after all, in public servants—she has a tremendous sense of right and wrong. That's what makes my trust in her considerable."

"She's rather pretty."

"She's not unattractive, I suppose. I'm so used to her I hardly notice."

"Odd that she hasn't married."

"She's devoted practically her whole life to public work."

Van der Valk concluded that it would be unfair to suspect the burgomaster of pinching Miss Burger's bottom.

On his way out he saw the burgomaster's wife hovering. She came out on the step with him, leaving the porch light out and almost closing the front door.

"He has no idea at all," Van der Valk said carefully. "Just behave normally with him."

"That's one relief, at least."

"The thing that our author knows about your husband—it was personal only to him, or did it concern you as well?"

Her voice in the dimness was uncomfortable.

"Er—just him. Myself only indirectly. I can't tell you, I'm afraid."

"No matter. Just one query more and I'll ask no further. Was it anything that would concern a doctor?"

"No." That ruled that out.

"Good night, Madame."

And now home.

7

Arlette was waiting for him. He had only once before seen her so pinched and tense—one night when he was four hours late and she knew that he was carrying a gun, a thing he did maybe once a year. Contrary to public belief, plain-clothes policemen ordinarily have no right to carry weapons.

"But what's the matter? I'm not very late. The garage was very slow."

She did not speak but, with a nervous shudder, held out a plain white envelope.

He was delighted. Yes, delighted. Never had he been so pleased.

"Is this what I think it is?"

"Yes."

"When did it come? And how?"

"In the mailbox. But I don't know when. It's been dark an hour. People put things in the box all the time. Children with pamphlets from shops—bargains, advertisements—sometimes two or three together."

"Anything else come?"

"As I said, just pamphlets."

"Did you keep them?"

"Why should I? I never do. You want them? In the basket in the kitchen" He scrabbled in the wastebasket. Yes, the local supermarket, with a banner headline about cheap vermouth and five cents off oatmeal, biscuits, and condensed milk till Saturday. A printed postcard inviting them to write for free details of extraordinarily cheap sewing machines. A little mimeographed circular reminding them that a very superior doctor of divinity would address interested persons next Tuesday at 7 P.M. Subject, "The Ecumenical Survival."

Mm.

The envelope was quite good quality, plain, unaddressed, had been sealed. He wondered whether it was worth while to run chemical tests on it.

"I half guessed," said Arlette miserably. "When I read it . . ." A violent shudder.

"It's aimed at you?" Curious, very curious—when all the other women had been local.

"As far as I can see, at both of us. Venomously indiscriminate."

He sat down in the living room and drew the paper out slowly.

"Bring both of us a drink. Just make sure the curtain are shut properly."

"I thought of that, too," bitterly. Fright, shock, disgust. She wasn't over it by any means; she poured two glasses of port and spilled some. However, the policeman had to come before the husband. Sorry, Arlette.

It was all he had wished, had longed for. And more. "The one of you is no better than the other. Hypocrites. An official from the Ministry—nosing in our affairs, looking down at us because we are plain honest people. How do you have the nerve to bring a woman with you—I should like to see her marriage papers.

"Foreign harlot—why don't you go back to whatever brothel in Paris you came out of? The women here are decent God-fearing people. They know that God watches them. God was watching you. Seeing a woman behave like that in our town.

"You call yourself a public servant. Pervert, abandoned, vicious. I have written to the Ministry in The Hague to denounce you to your superiors. Holland is utterly sunk in sin. But we know here what it is we have to fight. Get out and take your prostitute with you."

No spelling mistakes, and careful punctuation. Even a question mark had been carefully clipped and inserted. He wanted to jump about with enjoyment but he was sorry for Arlette. He gave her a broad smile.

"Very tame, after a few I've had. I'm unhappy that you had to see it first—but, you know, this was all I needed."

She drank some port and tried to grin back.

"Last night, when I got silly and did idiotic tricks with my garter belt—I got seen. My God, darling. Horrible."

"Listen to me. This is not the usual kind of letter, but it's clearly by the same writer. This is the ordinary two-for-a-nickel abusive kind, and a complete giveaway. She just couldn't resist the temptation to take a chance, wanting to show how clever she was. It'll hang her."

"Her?"

"That's a respectable housewife talking. Snub-nosed, corseted, popeyed, with thick wooden legs and a Sunday hat. She wears glasses and has arch supports inside her sensible laced shoes."

It was intended to make her laugh; he was glad to see it did.

"No, seriously, this is a woman. The writer of these letters isn't a man."

"A Lesbian, then? No wonder she didn't take to me."

"I think maybe a suppressed Lesbian."

"But according to the letters—"

"Ach, I think that was just talk. She may have booked some unexpected successes. Lots of these women—any women—have tendencies they wouldn't ordinarily dream of indulging or even formulating in conscious ideas. Men, after all, are pretty vile, mm? Here just as much as most places."

He drank his port with enjoyment.

"Have a look. Bursts wide open. Notice 'I have written to the Ministry.' Nobody, bar one or two, knows which Ministry I'm supposed to come from. The cards I've shown had no address—just a phony Institute of Studies.

"On the other hand, people I've interviewed know I'm from the police. This person knows too much and not enough. But it's not written with the head, to try and mislead me; the sentiments come from the heart, all right."

"I don't quite understand."

"Somebody who has access to knowledge, who has known all along what the police were doing, who hasn't thought of querying my identity. I came with official papers from the Ministry of the Interior. Nothing so compels a bureaucrat's utter faith as an official piece of paper."

"A bureaucrat—somebody from the municipal offices?"

"I've always thought that listening apparatus thing was baloney. I must admit I thought the peeking didn't exist, either—got caught there."

"But you said somebody who hated government interference. A bureaucrat—that is government interference."

"Two answers, I think. The government program started here with the new burgomaster; that's only five years or thereabouts. The one before was a local fellow and a complete dud. One could understand that anybody left over from the old regime might easily think that the municipality had got on perfectly well before the new brooms came.

"I can see that might be a reason, but it's hardly a motive."

"Just what bothered me. But the other reason is something Bescançon suggested. He remarked that a bureaucrat who turned against his cherished principles might become very dangerous. I thought of a judge in France, some few years ago, who went mad and burned his own courthouse down."

He could see Arlette looking at him dubiously. She was thinking, he guessed, that he, too, was a public servant—conscientious, even scrupulous sometimes, yet with revolutionary republican notions that had done him no good in the eyes of his superiors.

"Remarkable how I cannot detach Besançon from this business. Step by step, he has been inseparable from all my thinking about it."

"Yes, yes." Arlette was not much interested in

Besançon, whom she had never seen. Whereas this business touched her now personally. "I want to understand. What was it exactly he said that gave you this idea?"

"I asked him about the Hitler entourage. He distinguished between the fanatic idealists, the gangsters with simply egotistical motives, and the civil servants, who devotedly thought they were really serving the state. He suggested that if one of them were to see through it all, he would become the most unscrupulous and frightful of the lot. I can readily believe that. The ordinary ones were bad enough. Think of Eichmann —the pure civil servant."

"You mean you thought something of the sort existed here? Isn't that farfetched?"

"All my ideas are farfetched," he said ruefully. "I just thought of a bureaucrat who went crazy attacking the very institutions he'd always worshiped. It doesn't matter how I got the idea—if the psycho boys once start, they'll make the reports, and everybody believes them no matter how farfetched they choose to sound."

This was a Van der Valk grievance of long standing. He had seen it so often. If a policeman of years' experience came out with something like this in court, he'd be shoved straight out to graze in the meadows, whereas some little cocksure know-it-all doctor-boy who's read the books is listened to in religious silence. But he has learned—he would be cute enough to fill his report with bullshit about "Having narrowly observed the demeanor of the accused," and so on.

"I'm going out after supper. I still have to get some scrap of evidence that's tangible before I can ring the bell."

"But supper's ready. It has been for over half an hour. That wretched letter upset me so."

"Well, come on then. I'm hungry and I've a lot to do. One at a time, as the lion said when he ate the explorer's wife, too."

PART FIVE

CERTAINTY

1

PROWL—A BIG WORD. In a sense he was going to prowl. It was perfectly true that it is a good idea to have some proof before blowing the whistle. He hadn't any proof but he was pretty sure there would be plenty found under a search warrant. He didn't have to prowl.

Van der Valk had been told several times that he decorated things too much. It was true enough, he supposed. He was a creature of drama, and he liked doing ridiculous dramatic things. It wouldn't do any harm to prowl, though he felt quite sure now of his bird.

He wanted to walk about and meditate, too. He wanted open air and movement. This was a good excuse.

The weather was not encouraging. The snow had not lain, after all; it had started thawing in the afternoon. Now it was freezing again, with a thin mist, a vicious sharp wind that had backed into the north, and half-melted snow and ice blackened and rotting. He wasn't going out at night in that with his shiny-pants bureaucrat's suit on.

He put on shapeless corduroy trousers, a high-necked sweater, and a padded parka. Heavy shoes. Also a hat he was fond of; the brim came down all around—he looked like an English politician out grouse shooting. It was only at close quarters that he was detected and expelled from this august company —just a drunken gamekeeper, after all. He hadn't a shotgun but he took his binoculars. He thought that anybody who saw him would hardly identify this rural figure with the man from the Ministry, the student of ethnography, whatever that might be.

He went out the back door. The tiny back garden was nothing but neglected grass. Really, the municipal lawn mower would have to come and do it in the summer while he was doing the roadsides.

Windows glowed at him everywhere, oblong patches of brilliant light; hardly anybody had drawn curtains, even now. The windows were covered with condensation from the good old-fashioned Dutch fog that had been worked up within, but peeking was a simple affair to anybody who cared to make it his hobby. Television sets turned on, tea simmering, stove going full blast. Father deep in the local paper, Mother finishing her darning while champing on a biscuit and waiting for the Play to begin on the sacred screen, children finishing their homework. This piece, the legend would be flashed on presently, is "Not Suitable for Youthful Viewers." How true.

Nobody was out at this time—it was after eight-thirty—except the juvenile delinquents. And they weren't on the streets. They would be gathered in their café in the village, the motorbikes in an untidy heap outside and the juke box playing.

Van der Valk walked through the "suburbs" of the little town. A hodgepodge straggle, trying to keep up with the housing shortage and never succeeding; the same picture one finds everywhere in all Dutch towns, all German and Italian and Czech and Polish, and so on. Streets half finished, the raw beginnings of a park, skeletons of flats, piles of bricks and roof tiles lying around in the mud, warped wooden timbers and rusty scaffolding lying about in between to be tripped over. Every now and then the reminder of how much of a frontier town this still was struck sharply. Streets neat and trim and lived-in collapsed into rank moorland. There were fields of curly kale between the patches where foundations had been excavated, and square pits of dark earth lay half full of black water. A raw church of staring brick, no bells yet hanging in the gawky tower, was still surrounded on three sides by grazing cows.

Sensibly, the bog had been drained and landscaped at the start with dragline excavators, creating little hillocks and artificial lakes. Once these were clothed with a little greenery, they would be attractive, doubtless, but the clamor for housing was such that the plan had been patchworked, without continuity. Builders had put up houses whose roofs were already on while the pumps were still throwing dirty water out of the foundations, the workmen lurching stickily about in rubber boots, the contractors struggling vainly to keep up with the five-year plan that was to raise the population of Zwinderen to twenty thousand.

The streets were temporary affairs: zigzag courses of brick hammered in over a vaguely leveled belt of coarse rubble. Sketchily founded, half drained, they were pitted and jagged like a moon landscape. Full, too, of greasy black puddles, sudden death to high heels, and an unmerciful hammering to anything but a Land Rover or a Citroën. He was accustomed to all this by now, threading a way with automatic side steps where the blue or orange glare of a sparse street lamp warned one of the deepest, most treacherous pits.

Everything was still and quiet. Van der Valk passed one elderly man walking his dog, and was passed in turn by an ancient bicycle, its loose back fender rattling on the bumps, its uncertain front light wavering drunkenly. An erratic wind, wet and cold, blew at him from all quarters and was broken into a thousand drafts at every corner; the landscape was as eerie as the middle of a forest. He stopped suddenly, alert. What was that? Who was dodging about there? Nothing and nobody—a tarpaulin over a pile of builders' material was flapping to the gusts. "Frolic wind," he told himself sarcastically. "Zephyr, with Aurora playing"—ha.

The quotation suddenly clicked into place, giving him a reference he had been groping for—a book that had made some stir in the thirties. He remembered it because he had picked it up off a second-hand stall in a little old-maidish Surrey town where he had been billeted in wartime; it had made an amusing change from the army. *Frolic Wind* . . .

There had been a poet who had gone for a bath in the lily pond during a thundershower—lovely. And three crazy old sisters, one of whom lived in a tower, which she kept locked because all the walls were covered with obscene pictures she had painted. Lady Athaliah, that was it.

He leaned against a pile of bricks and fastened the binoculars on a block of flats a hundred yards off. Top corner flat, first and second windows at the northern angle. Lady Athaliah's tower? He twisted the wheel delicately and a brightly lit interior sprang into focus. Ha. He could see a head, and wanted to see more. But he was too low; even at this distance he couldn't see much of a second-floor room.

He looked about. Everything was dark and deserted where he was, with nothing finished yet; this was the program for next spring and summer. That second-floor window, with its patch of uncurtained lemon light, looked out upon a moon landscape. No passers-by. Except Van der Valk, with his little peep glass. He crossed the road and walked into a house that had a roof but no windows and no door. He hoped there would be floors. He smelled the acrid reek of wet cement, unseasoned wood, and white-lead priming paint, and groped up a little steep staircase, coming out in a cell of bare unplastered brick with a metal window frame stuck in the middle of it. The smell was the same, enriched by the builders, who had been piddling in the corner; they would. But the twelve feet up from street level made all the difference to his sight line; Peeping Tom now had an admirable view of the tower.

No satyrs or nymphs, alas, capering across the walls. Quite the contrary. The very ordinary, very conventional living of an unmarried woman living alone, who is fairly well off but frugal. No taste, plenty of

neatness, tidiness, fussiness. A limp picture of sheep
grazing on a moor, a few frilly ornaments, a neatly
polished radio with a vase of flowers standing on a
square crocheted mat. The inevitable tray with
painted coffee cups and ornate biscuit tin. A Calvinist
interior, bare, impersonal, dull. No books to be seen,
no frivolities. She led, of course, an active life, her
evenings occupied with pieties, committee sitting, visit-
ing newly settled families, bringing them into the fold,
enlisting them, too, in charitable social works.

But no committee was sitting this evening.

What on earth was Lady Athaliah wearing?

There were streaks and blurs of condensation on
the window; a whole panel of the view was obscured
by the potted plants ranged on the sill, but when she
moved he could see down to the waist—mm, reminiscent of one of the early films of Brigitte Bardot. He
moved into the corner of the window frame, banged
his elbow, cursed, shifted the glasses carefully, and
leaned out to get a better view, oblivious of everything
but that extraordinary robe affair.

Watching a person through binoculars—even if that
person is simply cleaning his teeth under the kitchen
tap—is a strong emotion. You are ashamed and excited. You are afraid, too, for it is like being in the
ring, watching the gloves that have hurt you and will
hurt you again, watching the eyes that may or may not
tell you the truth. And like looking over the sights of a
rifle; look, it lives and laughs, unconscious of my presence; it struts about, and one small twitch of my finger
will knock it ludicrously arse over teakettle into eternity and that dung heap. With binoculars you are the
submarine commander, the assassin, the preacher in

the pulpit, God. As well as, always, the pornographer.
A strong hot emotion.

Looking at Miss Burger through binoculars was
pornographic less perhaps because of that ridiculous
filmy negligee thing, which reminded one of nothing
so much as a brassière advertisement in a women's
magazine, than because it was so sad, and anything
pornographic is so hatefully sad.

She was very painted—her mouth and especially
her eyes, and that in itself was shocking. The clean
scrubbed face of a Dutch woman—and only a very
few years ago only whores, in Holland, were made up
—has no affinity to paint, and she had done it badly,
of course, overdramatically in colors that were far too
bright. After the painted face the naked body was less
shocking.

She was floating about, a cigarette in her mouth in
a long holder. Van der Valk wondered what she was
doing. He could see no other person in the room, but
her face was animated by speech; her lips moved. She
looked arch and grotesquely coquette. Then he saw it
was a seduction scene. A solitary seduction. He understood suddenly that in another five minutes she would
be making love to herself. And he was watching her
from a dark empty house with binoculars.

Something very villainous happened to him at that
moment. He wanted to see her. To see her below the
waist, he would have to climb on the roof. There
would be a ladder lying about, no doubt; he was suddenly in a tearing hurry to hunt for it.

To get to see her below the waist, he was ready to
hunt for a ladder and climb on the roof, was he? Now,
that was laughable.

The temptation of Saint Anthony was removed suddenly by a voice. A pretty rough voice, at that, and quite unsympathetic to the pornographic instincts.

"Hey!" it bellowed.

Considerably startled, Van der Valk lowered the glasses and glanced downward. With mixed feelings, he surveyed a uniformed policeman, standing burly and menacing beside his bike. The policeman was surveying right back, not at all with mixed feelings. Stupid of Van der Valk not to realize that of course they would patrol out here as well, where people often came to pinch the builders' materials.

"Caught red-handed, by God," said the rough voice. "Just what we've been looking for these six months." There was a snort—as near as a country policeman will get, in Holland, to a chortle, whatever that is—of self-congratulation. Van der Valk was quite regretful that he would have to spoil the fun. He took stock of his situation and felt extremely foolish.

"I'll come down the stairs," he said reasonably.

"No, you don't. Have you dodge out the back and make a run for it, eh? You stay there." To reinforce his argument, the policeman lugged his cannon into view. He didn't exactly point it at Van der Valk, but it was enough to make a fairly desperate criminal, like the Inspector, realize that the policeman meant what he said.

"Now, throw the glasses, clever fellow—underhand, gently. Thanks. That's evidence, see? And now you drop out on the ground. It's not high; you won't hurt yourself. Not that I'd care if you did."

There was no earthly use in talking. Van der Valk gripped the sill meekly, swung his legs out, lowered, loosened, and did a parachutist's jump onto sodden earth. The grimy black ground stuck disagreeably to his palms, and he wiped them on the corduroy trousers. That would irritate Arlette, who would doubtless otherwise think the whole thing extremely funny. To be pinched for a peeper by the municipal constabulary!

"And now march. I'm right behind you. I need one hand to wheel my bike, but I won't hesitate to fire if you break."

Van der Valk marched. At the corner of the main road into the town a police Volkswagen van came touring past.

"Hoi!" went his guardian angel.

The van stopped and a head poked out.

"What you got there?"

"Just guess."

"Not the one that set the builders' hut on fire?"

"Forget the hut, forget the fire. The sex maniac."

"Ho."

"Pinched him in the act, spying in an empty house." He waved the binoculars triumphantly.

"Ho." Impressed. "We'll hear all about it when we get back."

"March," said the angel.

Van der Valk sniffed the familiar police-bureau smell with affection. This had its comic side; he was beginning to enjoy himself.

"Now," said the duty brigadier pompously, settling a form between his elbows. "Name? . . . Christian names? . . . Address? . . . Profession?"

"Inspector of police."

"You better not try to be funny."

"Have a look in my pocket," Van der Valk said reasonably, and at once got a sinking feeling—he had changed, and hadn't emptied his pockets. "No, I've just realized I haven't any identity papers on me."

"Haw."

"I'm serious." It was less funny; he had to make an effort. "You can send the wagon around and ask my wife to give you the papers?"

"Why bother? You're staying here; you're for the cell."

"Look, if I'm kidding you, you'll hit me on the head with a cannon, and it does me no good. I know perfectly well you'll keep me here. But when you don't check my identity and I'm not kidding, you'll be in trouble."

"Police where?" Skeptical. "Fairyland?"

"Central Recherche, Amsterdam."

"Haw. What happened, then? You go for a walk in the dark and lose your way, or what?"

Anything he said would have added to the comedy, so he kept his mouth shut and gave the policeman his big, frank, open grin. The policeman looked him up and down very carefully then. Van der Valk could see that he wasn't only studying him, but had been listening attentively to the sound of his voice. Then his captor reached for the mobilophone transmitter key and buzzed it.

"Jan? Whereabouts are you? . . . Well, drive over to the Mimosastraat. Number twenty-five. If there's a woman there, you tell her that her husband's held here, and to give you his identity papers—and they'd better be convincing. O.K.? . . . Yes, right away."

There was a wait of a quarter of an hour. The brigadier doodled on the back of his form. Van der Valk's angel breathed heavily through his nose. Nobody stopped Van der Valk from smoking. And there was no light conversation.

He heard the noisy motor of the minibus, a squeal of brakes, followed by exaggerated door-slamming. Arlette, possibly, had been sarcastic and they were taking it out on the car.

There she was in person, looking determined, marching in advance of a faintly ruffled bodyguard.

"What did you bring her for, Jan?"

"She brought us."

"Oh."

"I'm sure all the neighbors are delighted?" Van der Valk asked, catching the wallet she tossed him.

"Hanging out the windows, buzzing like a beehive."

"Bitte sehr," Van der Valk said, presenting the desk man with his police identity card and his extra-duty authorization, signed by the Procureur-Général. The desk man read all of it, chagrin tinged with awe.

"Sorry."

"Not your fault. I changed, forgot my wallet, and you saw me in peculiar circumstances." He gave the company commander's look of stern authority, taking in, in the semicircle, four openmouthed policemen.

"Look—sir—I'll have to ring up the inspector and tell him."

"Yes. He'll have to know right away. And I'll have a bit of business for him myself, I think."

With no great enthusiasm, the desk man reached for his telephone.

"The case is finished," Van der Valk said to Arlette. "I'll stay here, now that I am here, because there'll be a lot of paper work. I'll have to explain to the inspector what's been going on. Got a bit out of hand. Do you mind—going back to the Mimosastraat, I mean?"

"Not at all. I can start packing. I'll be delighted. And whatever the neighbors are thinking, it no longer bothers me."

"It's a pity we haven't had a bit more of that spirit." Van der Valk fixed the car patrol, which was still somewhat openmouthed, with a glittering eye. "These kind gentlemen will give you a lift."

2

The inspector of police in Zwinderen was not pleased at being rung up and dragged away in the middle of the Play, which was exciting, with gangsters. Still less was he pleased with Van der Valk's invasion of his territory. Least of all with having been kept in the dark.

"I'm sorry about it, too. But please realize that I'm under orders. It wasn't my idea, and I've never liked it, either. It seems the Procureur-Général himself decided that nobody was to know except the burgomaster. Total security, because of the leak over there, see?"

"Miss Burger—good grief. I see her pretty nearly every day."

"That's one reason at least—and not the worst, either—why nobody ever suspected her. When you were on this affair initially, she must have known everything you said, though, or did. Huh? Hardly surprising that you never found out. Who would, under those conditions?"

He nodded heavily. "Assen hammed it up, too."

"Not to speak of the State Recherche."

"They went on at me as though there were a hole you could drive a bus through in my organization."

Van der Valk knew that he had asked for a transfer, because a State Recherche investigation looked like too much of a reflection on him. The burgomaster had talked him out of it—it was in the confidential file. Van der Valk felt a good deal of sympathy with him.

"Ach," Van der Valk said, "now it can soon be finished. It's only ten-thirty—you could pick her up right away. We're pretty certain to find all the evidence we'll need in her flat."

"And suppose there's nothing?"

"She'll talk to you. You see, I saw her; that will upset her. She won't love me—here under false pretenses." For Arlette's sake, Van der Valk would keep quiet about the letter he had in his pocket. The other woman, too, might possibly be grateful to have that forgotten.

"You don't think a summons— No, I can see it has to be an arrest, and the sooner the better." He got up and put his head out of the door. "Haas!"

"Sir." An oldish three-striper; solid, impressive, with a lot of jaw. He looked very quiet, a good man for a disagreeable job.

"Haas, I want a woman arrested now, tonight, without noise, with tact and patience. I want the warrant executed by you."

"Sir."

"You'll take the little car. Don't lose sight of her; she may do something unbalanced."

"And if she has to dress, sir?"

"Damn it, Haas, I don't have to teach you police procedure at your time of life, do I?"

"Sir."

Van der Valk was amused; it was one of the classic problems posed for the police cadets by the instructor on "Relations with the Public":

"You are instructed to arrest a woman suspected of being a jewel thief in her hotel room, at night. You have been warned to avoid disturbance. When asked to accompany you to the bureau, the woman refuses to dress. She threatens 'with immense relish' to scream, tear her nightdress, complain that you made indecent proposals to her, bruise her face, and claim that you used violence. What steps will you take?"

"But why?" the inspector said suddenly to the closed door. "Of all people."

"I suppose we might find something in her past. Childhood, upbringing, early experiences. Not police work, thank heaven."

"I have heard, I think, that she was an orphan."

"If she was brought up in a state orphanage, that might account for a few things."

"Psychology," with deep distaste.

"It'll all take months, no doubt. Compulsion toward public service, resentment of governmental inflexibility. Meticulous, perfectionist neurosis. Wound up with sex and strong religious feelings. Shame and horror at Lesbian inclinations, which she tries to work off in social work; only makes it worse—hell, I'm just guessing." The inspector was a local man; Van der Valk wasn't going to brush the man's hair the wrong way by going into his notions of the Calvinist wish for isolation, independence, putting the clock back, or his feeling that to wrestle against sin with a Calvinist conscience was not the best method to cure emotional instability.

"The burgomaster'll be upset—he thinks the world of her."

"But only as a public servant. I guess she got sick of being a cog and wanted someone who would think the world of her as a person. What does it matter?"

"Not to us, anyway, now we've got the criminal."

"We've got another victim," Van der Valk corrected mildly.

3

Miss Burger did not make a scene with chief agent of police Haas, a man she had known all her life. But when she saw Van der Valk, she went into hysterical tears and used four-letter words. They hadn't found the listening gadget—she denied ever having heard of it and it remained a mystery—but they found the Bardot robe that Van der Valk had seen her in, walking about playing her pathetic part. And they found an envelope with cut-up newsprint.

Everybody asked how Van der Valk had thought of her. He had prepared his answer. She had had access to all kinds of information, he said smoothly, and had developed a passion for having a finger in everything. In her spare-time activities she had met and talked with all the women that had received letters. What had made her write imaginary abuse of their husbands was none of his affair. The Protestant minister, he thought, had what had seemed to her dangerously modernist leanings. Van der Valk glossed over a good deal, and did not mention the burgomaster's wife. He said he had never believed much in the creeping around at night—tried it myself, he said jocularly, and promptly got pinched by the very efficient municipal police. This greatly soothed the still-ruffled inspector. Van der Valk did not say that both his wife and he had found out in a disagreeable way that she did creep about at night.

The burgomaster, rung up, was very concerned though relieved. If, Van der Valk reflected, the burgomaster had known about his wife, he would be more of both. Maybe she would tell him when it all leaked out.

Will would be happy that no one had said nasty things about his sister-in-law.

The director of the milk factory, freed from the accusation of being too friendly with his great healthy shiny farm girls, would be happy.

The minister would be reinstated; they might manage to cure his wife.

And Mr. Besançon would doubtless be happy when he heard that there was no longer any need to suspect him of heaven knew what. It could not have been pleasant for him, the owlish suspicions of relays of policemen.

Of course, someone who shuns society and is not enthusiastic about his fellow citizens of the twentieth century is asking for a bad name in Holland. Land of community activities, of jolly clubby get-togethers on

the slightest pretext. Our Treasurer is this week twelve
and a half years married. Our Secretary has for fifteen
uninterrupted, productive, endless years been the very
cornerstone of Municipal Sanitation.

Even Van der Valk had suspected Besançon, and
still didn't know what of.

Van der Valk got home at about three in the morning, his paper work done. There would be, of course,
a detailed report for Mr. Sailer in Amsterdam, but
that could wait till he was home. Arlette, he was glad
to see, had already done the packing. Not that there
was very much. About what one would have for a holiday; a couple of weeks in beautiful unspoiled Drente.

He would have to make a courtesy call on the burgomaster in the morning.

Who would do all the little jobs like finding accom-
modation for officials, now that Miss Burger was due
for a rest in a clinic? Dear, dear, the municipal administration would be in an uproar, with its invaluable
can-do department vanished.

4

"If you have a courtesy call to make," said Arlette—
she had not lit the stove and they were standing
chilled, clutching inadequate coffee cups to their bos-
oms—"it'll just leave me time to get the house as tidy
as we found it. Your Miss Burger may be off her
rocker—I have to admit I felt sorry for the woman—
but she was good at her job."

"Too good. She must have been under tremendous
tension. That need to do everything, know everything

—the perfectionist urge, being meticulous in the tiniest details—is a classic pointer, or was when I went to school."

"You mean that you're glad I'm sloppy and forget things?" said Arlette rather meanly.

Van der Valk suspected that the burgomaster had, after all, learned something from his wife, remembered his questions, and drawn conclusions. He was full of warm compliments, nearly fulsome. Perhaps he was just extremely delighted to see Van der Valk's back. He promised that his own report would go off that very day to the Minister of the Interior, who would doubtless pass it on to Mr. Sailer.

"I've stolen our secretary's girl"—with a ghost of a smile—"but I'm afraid she'll never be nearly as good as Miss Burger. Her mind's too much on her boyfriend."

"Yes," Van der Valk said, grinning, unable to resist it, "I'm all for abnormality myself."

He walked off and left the bureaucrats hard at it, making a tiny market town in Drente into an industrial town with model garden suburbs, a place of beauty and joy to live in.

Arlette had the suitcases in the car. The neighbors were taking a great interest in her movements, and Mrs. Tattle at the back had bustled across with her inimitable blend of helpful nosiness. Van der Valk had no doubt that the theory was that he had been sacked for a misdemeanor, after being arrested by the police in disgraceful circumstances most unbefitting to a functionary of some obscure Ministry. He tried to see himself as a devoted servant of Ag and Fish, and remembered a delightful Frenchman he had once known, whose family had been in Ponts et Chaussées for five generations and who was now a painter in Santiago, Chile.

"One last call I still want to make," Van der Valk said, crowding in behind the wheel. He was tall and fairly broad, and was wearing a winter overcoat; in a little Volkswagen one often has that moment of thinking the zipper won't close. "I think I should drop in on Besançon. Tell him the affair is officially closed. He stands in a peculiar position—he was number 1 suspect for months and I never have understood why. I've suspected him myself. And it's not just because he's odd, or a Jew. There's something almost sinister about the man. Perhaps you'll see it."

"I'll be interested to see him, anyway, after hearing him spoken about so much."

"Quite apart from business, I like him. I've found myself getting friendly with the old boy," he said, stopping the car at Besançon's gate.

"This is my wife."

"Honored, Madame." Besançon had his neutral, indifferent voice, but he made a formal Germanic bow and kissed her hand with politeness.

"No, thanks, we won't sit down. We're just dropping in to say goodbye."

"Really? Your affair is untangled?"

"It is. You won't be pestered by any more policemen, I should imagine. Certainly not by me. In Amsterdam they'll all say I've wasted enough time and I'd better get back to work." The strange look crossed

Besançon's face for an instant, the look that Van der Valk had seen the first time he had met him, and told him he didn't really think he had been writing crazy letters. Van der Valk had thought then that it might be relief. He still thought so. He didn't know, though.

"Another eccentric elderly man like myself?"

"No, no—an overzealous constipated female civil servant with a Calvinist conscience."

Besançon smiled faintly. "I seem to recall that we touched on the point in conversation. Didn't I tell you that the born civil servant is a dangerous person?"

"You did. And I think the remark helped me more than I care to admit. I haven't exactly been a shining example of deductive or even intuitive intellectual brilliance around here."

"You must allow me to offer you both a drink."

"Thanks, but we've a long drive ahead. I do want to say that it has been a pleasure talking to you—I can't in honesty say knowing you, because I don't. It was one of the few things that gave me pleasure while I was here, and I'm very grateful."

"You are more than kind," formally. He looked at Arlette, who was wearing her llama jacket and looking pretty. "I have been pleased to meet you, Madame, and regret only that it should be brief. But I am not old enough not to expect pleasures."

"That's even nicer for me than for you, because I certainly don't expect to give them." Her accent was strong this morning.

He gave her his tired, faint smile, but something had moved him; the lines on the still, hard face altered for a second.

"You recall my wife to me strongly." It was only an instant; he corrected himself at once.

"I quite agree, a remarkable man," Arlette said a mile farther on.

"Very. I can't reach bottom at all with him. All sorts of depths. Even his books tell me little enough." Arlette knew that Van der Valk had a passion for the book test; he had sometimes boasted, unwisely, that he could make a character assessment from a library.

"He professes no interest in religion, but he has a Bible on his desk. He dislikes live Jews, but likes dead ones. What were the others he had there? Yes, a biography of Cromwell and the plays of Corneille. An interest in conscience? The conflict between emotion and duty—the classical dilemma? I've no idea."

Arlette was not interested in Corneille. "Who is Cromwell? The name is vaguely familiar."

"A seventeenth-century English De Gaulle," Van der Valk said rather frivolously. "Very interesting— the Puritan conscience at its finest. The Sword of the Lord. Submitted himself completely to God, did what God told him, and, once he was satisfied he knew what God wanted, utterly immovable. Good cavalry general, and a very good politician. But rather an odd study, one might think, for a Jewish atheist watchmaker with a nervous degeneration disease after five years in the Third Reich."

"He can't be an atheist, I should think."

"Perhaps he's become a Calvinist," Van der Valk said, still frivolously.

"Watch your cigarette."

"Sorry. I have to keep both eyes on the road; it's

slippery. And no books about Jews or Jewry at all, unless you count *Jud Süss,* which is only a novel, if a good one."

"Not about Jews anyway."

"Come. Wonderful rabbis, fearful eighteenth-century moneylenders."

"I only meant the man isn't really a Jew at all, hm? Pretends to be a Jew."

"Not pretends—decides to be a Jew." Van der Valk lapsed into silence; the road was very slippery in patches.

5

With a huge sigh of pleasure Arlette opened her own front door. "Only dust. Once the stove's lit and a drink poured out, we're home."

"Where are the plants?"

"Old Mother Counterpoint has them." That was the old lady on the ground floor who gave piano lessons, a dear old lady. Arlette was fond of her, especially as they were agreed that Samson François was the only pianist in the world who could play Debussy.

"A drink quick."

"There's some cognac left from Zwinderen. In the brown case with the broken lock. Careful—it's only held by the strap."

"To Drente."

"And may we never have to go back."

They went to bed early. Van der Valk was tired, but he lay awake a long while. Reaction, he told himself.

He went next day to the office, where a good deal of humor, intended as wit, was fired at him. His boss

—that old maid Commissaris Tak—was inclined to approve of him, for once.

"I'm bound to say you've wasted no excessive amount of time. You're due, in justice, some time off. Mm, today's Friday. Take the weekend, which is yours anyhow. I'll expect you Monday morning."

It sounded generous, but the weekend was Van der Valk's anyway. Tak was good at the trick of making a regulation sound like generosity.

"You'll have to make a report to the Palais."

"I'll be doing that over the weekend."

But instead of going home—if he didn't get out quick, Tak would get a phone call, fly up the wall, and call him back—Van der Valk sat in his office for ten minutes, brooding. His colleague was out working; he had it to himself. At the end of the ten minutes he picked up the intercom telephone that links all the offices in the headquarters building.

"Morning, Klaas."

"Hey, you back? What's new?"

"Tell you over a beer."

"No time today."

"Monday maybe. I wanted to know the phone number of the Jewish bureau in Vienna."

"You don't need it. One right here in Amsterdam. They'll phone Vienna for you if they don't happen to have what you want. Don't tell me you're mixed up with that racket?"

"I'm mixed up in all the rackets," Van der Valk said ruefully. "What's the address?"

Dr. Eli Lazarus was a mild fat man, who looked as though his greatest enemy were no more than the fe-

male malaria mosquito. He showed no outward signs
of damage; he had a smooth unwrinkled baby face
with a sad joviality about it, like an intellectual come-
dian. But he had lost anywhere up to a hundred rela-
tives in the camps—every single person he possessed.
Like Besançon, like hundreds and thousands more.
Can one accuse people like that of losing their integ-
rity, their balance, their inner peace? Who knew—it
was Besançon all over again—what happened to the
mentality of people who had spent years in the "dust-
bin of the Reich," as Heydrich jokingly called it. Exactly like Besançon, Dr. Lazarus belonged to another
world; one could not reach the depths of a man like
that.

He was one of the mild, implacable, kind, reasonable monomaniacs who have sworn never to rest until
the last German or Slav or just plain man accused of
genocide has been brought to justice. Van der Valk
found it a peculiar sensation just being in his office;
abominable crimes were filed here the way the employment bureau filed plumbers and salesgirls. Murder,
torture, sterilization, enforced prostitution, infection
with moral disease—you name it, he'd got it.

"In a certain sense, we're near the end of our
tether," he was saying in the quiet earnest voice of a
man dedicated to Pre-Cambrian fossils. "We have
accounted for nearly all the persons against whom
we have any hope of bringing convincing evidence.
Experience has shown us that not even the Superior
Court in Karlsruhe can get a conviction without witnesses. I do not mean the silent witnesses—I mean
men and women who can still appear, speak, exercise
the power of words—'I saw, I heard, I have felt.'

There were so terribly few, and now, fifteen years after . . ." He rested his big double chin on a square firm hand.

"And what remains?"

"There remains a large—painfully large—file of persons whom we know perfectly well. We know their identity, we know their shocking history, and we know that they sometimes quite cynically admit everything that we could accuse them of. But we have no juridical grip upon them. We find it impossible to bring them to trial simply for lack of the compelling evidence I have mentioned."

"It is no longer enough to say 'I accuse'?"

"It is not enough."

"And the real higher-ups? The top few, whose names are known to the whole world? Like the one who killed himself last year in Egypt, the one who is supposed to be in Paraguay? The ones that have remained lost or hidden up till now?"

A faint smile twitched at Dr. Lazarus' big shaved jaw.

"Are you falling into the temptation of the treasure hunt, Mr. Van der Valk?"

"You mean the well-known secrets of the Töplitz See?"

"Not exactly, though that is as good an example as any. While the Austrian authorities were diving for those so-called treasures, we were pestered with a wasps' nest of rumor. Every well-publicized figure of those times was placed by countless eyewitness tales within a thousand yards of that lake. Every hoary legend got a new lease on life. Even Skorzeny, who was quietly in Spain and is, in any case, no criminal at all. Even Müller, hardiest and most persistent legend of all."

"Tell me."

"The treasure hunt, Mr. Van der Valk, consists largely of following up people who say they have seen Müller. It happens constantly. Only today we have a long tale that he is directing the secret police in Albania. It is and remains a chronic obsession."

"And what do you know for certain about Müller?"

"For certain, not even if he is alive at all. We have followed innumerable false trails, some of which seemed remarkably authentic, so great is the aura, the sort of evil romance, that surrounds Müller's name. Who—tell me—can come to me and claim he has even a remote notion what Müller looks like? There exist descriptions, photographs, you might answer. I will reply that these photographs and descriptions are of anybody and everybody. I could go here with you into the street and, in a quarter of an hour, point out to you twenty Müllers—a streetcar conductor, a clerk at the Bourse, the teller of your bank."

"I see."

"We know, of course, certain facts, such as those that enabled us to examine the grave in Berlin, but we cannot say, 'That is the man.' And we have said, so many times, 'That is not the man.' Müller defeats us —on that plane. Further, there are curious inconsistencies in all the accounts—contemporary accounts, you understand—of the man's actions, behavior. To take one of the classic examples, a British officer, Captain Best, who was interrogated by Müller. He mentions the features that have become cliché—

the eyes, the shouting, and so on—and then remarks
pleasantly, 'I found him rather a decent little man.'
We do, of course"—dryly—"have evidence of the
contrary."

"And is there nothing, then, to do?"

"We wait. As we do with many more. Evidence has
been secured against people whose cases were given
up as hopeless. After so many years, some of these
persons have felt sufficiently secure—and, I should
add, sufficiently protected—to creep out into the
open. They range"—with a ferocious irony—"from
farm laborers in Schleswig-Holstein to the directors of
old people's homes."

"I am very grateful to you, Dr. Lazarus."

"I am at your disposal. Should you find, in the
course of your duties (as, if I have understood the
purpose of your visit, you may guess you can find),
the tiniest of facts that may fit into a larger pattern, do
not hesitate to apply to me. But let me warn you
against becoming obsessed by the treasure hunt.
There are many, many, many men, less widely
known, with whom justice could be just as summary."

"Even if you caught Müller, you could not hang
him twice."

"Just so, Inspector. Müller has publicity value.
Which can be a decided handicap to us, as we discovered in the case of Eichmann."

"And if you never catch him?" Van der Valk was
interested in Dr. Lazarus. It seemed that Müller would
never rest in peace, that his life's work could never
be done.

He looked at Van der Valk thoughtfully, weighing

what answer he should give him. "I take it, Inspector, that you believe in the justice of God?"

"I do. I am, however, a paid professional servant of a very inadequate, pathetically incompetent human justice."

"My answer to your question might well be your answer, Inspector."

"I might possibly answer that I did not know—nor could I know—what punishments, human punishments, have visited such a man."

"And have you developed that argument?"

"It is neither my task nor my right."

"Nor mine."

Van der Valk reflected, on the way home, that Dr. Lazarus had spent years in the camps. He was a doctor of medicine, and of parapsychology. He knew a great deal about law. And he knew what it was like to have no person left in the world. He would be quite an expert on punishments.

Whereas Van der Valk was a bum inspector of police, an expert on asking rag-and-bone men to show their pushcart license. An expert, perhaps, on rag-and-bone men.

He couldn't eat his dinner.

He couldn't explain to Arlette.

He opened a drawer, strapped on a shoulder holster, put a pistol in it, shrugged his shoulders, and put the whole lot back.

He thought of everybody he knew. He knew a Jewish doctor who was a neurologist. He knew the Procureur-Général. He knew a few retired policemen. He had read a lot of books, some of them by writers who knew a good deal about people. He stared at his

bookshelves. Mauriac, Simenon, Flaubert. Charles de
Foucauld. Saint Theresa, Büchner, Dostoevski, Ra-
cine, the *Memorial of Saint Helena*.

Either there weren't enough books or he hadn't
read them properly.

Nobody could help him, not even Arlette.

He muttered something at her, took a streetcar to
the Central Station, and got on a train that smelled
very nasty indeed of stale cheap cigar smoke and im-
perfectly washed humanity that has a prejudice
against open windows.

He thought about Corneille and Oliver Cromwell.

The only person he could think of in the whole
world who might be able to help him was S.S. Lieutenant General Heinrich Müller. Whose grave was in
Berlin. Written on it "To our beloved father."

Dr. Lazarus, or one of his friends, had come along
busily looking at bones and said the back teeth were
wrong. Anyway, the bones of several people were in
the grave.

Perhaps Mr. Müller had had no objection at the
time to company.

6

In Drente it was dry, and the night air felt warm, with
a gentle westerly breeze. Van der Valk had the idea
the sun had been shining all day. This was all wrong.
It was supposed to get warmer as one went south and
nearer sea—and in Amsterdam the streets had been
full of greasy half-frozen slush, the air at or below
freezing point, and the sky trying hard either to

snow or to rain and achieving neither beyond a foul
misty drizzle.

He walked from the station, in Zwinderen. Nobody
looked at him. He got to the lunatic asylum and
wondered whether they'd been brave enough to put
Burger there. No such luck, probably; they would
more likely let her languish for months, poor bitch, in
the House of Keeping in Assen.

He rang at the gate, and pretty soon he heard the
slow, shuffling, but still firm footstep across the brick
path. The eyes glanced through the gap in the barri-
cade; when they saw him, a great jump of nerves went
across the whole face like electricity—a spark that
penetrated the powerful facial muscles, the dark
glasses, all the insulation.

"Forgive me, I failed for a second to recognize you.
But come in. A pleasant surprise. I suppose there is
some detail that has been forgotten, that you have
come back to fill in a few more forms?" He was talking too much, too.

"That's about it," vaguely.

Van der Valk sat down in the accustomed place,
the creaky cane armchair. Besançon sat at his desk,
hands folded in his lap, head and shoulders bowed.
Like that, he was an insignificant little man.

Van der Valk had no idea what to say; a silence
grew that was almost as complete as the one he had
broken into.

"A detail," he said at last with an effort, "that must
be repaired. I am often very stupid."

"I have never yet had that impression."

"You don't know me that well, General," Van der
Valk said in German. It was funny; he had a sort of

embarrassment. He was unable to say right out, "You are a notorious man; the execrated, the fearful, the larger-than-life." Quite right. This man was not any of those things. This was an aging, tired, frightened, dying man.

"Your German has a Hamburg sound, it seems to me."

"I was stationed there—nearly a year. In 1945. It's not good."

"I understand what you say well enough."

"I thought you would."

He straightened his shoulders, lifted his head; Van der Valk began to recognize the man he knew. The voice got its timbre back, its sardonic tone.

"I would like only to disclaim the 'General.' Napoleon created Marshals of France and the Empire; they were right to keep their titles. I have never had the slightest use for this one. Since at last, apparently, I have a name, use it."

"I might, if I knew what to say."

"You came, I take it, to do, not just to say."

"I don't know what to do, either."

He looked at Van der Valk. He got up then, shuffled slowly across the room—Van der Valk could see he missed his stick—and brought his brandy bottle and two glasses. He offered one to the Inspector, who took it. They clinked together solemnly, two men separated by everything and by nothing.

"You're drinking, then?" Van der Valk said stupidly.

"I am forbidden alcohol, yes. What importance has it? I shall, in any case, not live long."

Van der Valk suddenly got an extremely silly idea,

which startled him. "This brandy's not poisoned, is it?"

That got Besançon's ironical smile. "I had thought my melodramatic days were over. I possess no poisons. I have no wish to kill myself; I have no interest even in killing you."

"Yet I have told no one I was coming here." Do I wish to tempt him, Van der Valk thought. Why did I say that?

"I think I understand."

"I dare say that I could, quite easily, disappear. Not even my wife knows where I am."

"Are you suggesting that I should disappear?"

"Would it help?"

"No longer."

"You'd rather go in front of a tribunal?"

"At least I should not defend myself with excuses. Like Eichmann. The eternal subordinate. The man was always, you know, something of a fool. A competent fool."

"I don't think it ever occurred to anyone to bother whether he was a fool," Van der Valk said, perhaps too sarcastically.

"Is that what you propose doing? To hand me to the Jews? Whom I persecuted, killed? Whose identity, finally, I stole? It would be more than just."

"I don't want to be more than just. And I must not be less."

"You simply don't know," looking straight at Van der Valk.

"No."

"Why?"

"I don't think I should ever understand. Even if you told me. I don't want any confessions. I could not grasp it. You have done things enormous, unbelievable. Legend has exaggerated your exploits to a degree where I can't take them seriously. I can only see you as you are. A retired civil servant with a nervous illness. A man I have known, spoken to, shaken hands with, clinked glasses with. A man I like. Or is that Besançon?"

"Perhaps," gravely.

"I should prefer to have had none of these experiences."

"I understand."

"The real Besançon, I take it—"

"Is buried in the grave in Berlin."

"He resembled you closely?"

"Very. Looking at us together, one could not tell which was the Jew. Bormann, one day, made a coarse joke about it."

"You had planned it for a long time?"

"I planned"—impassively—"to steal him. Which I did."

"Your family knows?"

"No." Van der Valk left it at that.

"It was noticed here that you shunned the company of women. It was thought by some a suspicious circumstance."

He laughed, quite ordinarily, pleasantly.

"Why do you laugh?"

"I had told myself, you see, that I would keep a sort of fidelity to my wife. I was—I am—what is called a good family man. That, it seems, has drawn attention to me. When I had no other fidelities. Not to myself, to my country, to my state, to my function, to my absurd leader. To nothing." He held his open hands up as though to show Van der Valk that they contained nothing. He laid them then on the table, flat, loose, watching the trembling with a sort of curiosity.

It was good French cognac. Written on the label was "Fournisseur à Sa Majesté le Roi de Suède." He had given the Inspector a generous glass, too. Perhaps it gave him false courage.

"Tell me, then. What did you do?"

"What happens to civil servants, Inspector Van der Valk, who come to the conclusion that their government has betrayed them? They commit treason. Himmler, that idealist, tried to bargain with the Americans. I was more clear-sighted. I had understood the meaning of Yalta, of Casablanca. Germans alone could save Germany. It was too late; we had committed too many crimes." Van der Valk thought the man had forgotten he was there. He had passed into his familiar train of thought, from which there was no outlet. He had perhaps been mad—he was no longer so, and he doubted whether it ever had been so. He had deceived himself with mass hysteria, and remained too discerning to believe in it. He had taken refuge in the peculiar German cloudiness and confusion of thought that accompany German orderliness and efficiency, and found his thought refused to cloud; the merciful opacity of Himmler had eluded him. Everything had failed him, one after another. The mystique of the Administration, of the Fatherland, of the Leader— all had crumbled and collapsed.

He had looked, no doubt, for every possible excuse. When he had seen what crimes he had committed in the name of his sacred department, he had tried to quiet his torments by embarking on wilder, more fantastic, more dreadful crimes than ever. He had fallen into the myth of predestination, believing—for a while—that he had been sent as a scourge, himself damned, but elected by God to lie heavy on the necks of his fellow men.

He had clung to every excuse as long as he had been able. His mind had forced him inexorably to abandon one after another.

Finally he had found that his was the most odious name in Europe. Every human being was alert for the blood of Gestapo Müller. All his intelligence and force had been called up to save his pride. What did they know; what could they understand, those peasants? Americans, English, Russians—his contempt for them was as great as had been his contempt for Germans, for Jews. He was not going to defend himself, justify himself. And he wasn't going to be caught, to be ignominiously butchered. God would save Müller.

God had. Ever since, he had wondered why.

Instead of death and possible expiation—peace— he had been allowed to live. He disdained the network of underground sympathizers. Fools and criminals.

He did not dare even to trust his family. God had sent him a slow, mortal disease, as though to say to him, "You have still time." But God had not affected his intelligence.

"A man will cling to his life," Van der Valk heard himself saying.

"I agree. Even Müller. During the long periods of interrogation, I thought daily that I would be discovered. How many times have I wanted to scream, to say, 'Fools, fools, can you not see what is under your

nose?' They accepted me as a Jew. For years I stayed
here, wondering what was required of me. Then the
police came again. Not to demand a reckoning from
Müller, but to know whether a crazy old Jew had written obscene letters to respectable Dutch housewives.
The irony of it. I lived in daily fear, but I still clung to
my life. It is all I have left. It is worth remarkably little. You have come to take it. You are the one who,
accidentally, has discovered the secret that all Europe
has hunted for."

Van der Valk did not care for the idea that he was
the instrument chosen by God to bring Gestapo Müller to justice. What justice? Justice, with somebody
who has committed crimes like these, does not exist.
They put Eichmann in a glass case and played out a
long, odious, humiliating farce. It did the Jews no
good, the world no good. Did it do Eichmann good? It
was not Van der Valk's job to decide that. They had
to hang him; they had no choice. What battle had
gone on in the mind of the President of Israel before,
with a sigh, he had signed the paper that released
the trap door?

Van der Valk was furious with the chance—
chance?—that had brought him face to face with this
man.

Surely Müller was coming to the inescapable conclusion that what was wanted of him was a voluntary
surrender to a will that was not his. Free will is the
most important thing we have. Van der Valk refused
to be a predestined agent for the arrest of Müller.

"Damn you," Van der Valk said. "I should take
you outside and shoot you, with no more ado than I
would give a sheep-killing dog."

"That is quite natural," he said in Besançon's voice.

"Both dramatic and handy," Van der Valk said sourly. He was not happy at this seeming inability to do anything at all.

"You are a bad policeman," thoughtfully, wearily.

"I have never realized it more completely than now."

"We have at least self-knowledge in common. I will help you, by telling you a story."

"Go ahead," dully.

"It was decided to provoke a frontier incident that would give pretext for an invasion of Poland. A man called Müller was entrusted with this. He gave the operation the name 'Canned Goods'—being a fellow of humor. He arranged for half a dozen condemned criminals to be transported to a selected border post where there was a communication center of no importance. The criminals were given injections, dressed in German uniforms, and shot while unconscious, to give a picture of a Polish attack." He paused, and gave Van der Valk a smile that belonged to Müller— the Müller that thought of the name "Canned Goods" —rather than to Besançon.

"I have had no injections, of course. But I am dying as surely as though I had. And I am a condemned criminal."

Van der Valk found his hands trembling. Like Müller's. If he had a gun, he thought, he would shoot this man—here, on the spot. Who would ever know?

Müller reached down slowly, opened the drawer of his table, and put a pistol on the desk between them. Van der Valk stared at the pistol.

"I took considerable pains to acquire that. I have

often been tempted to use it. But I have had too much pride."

The tension broke; Van der Valk felt himself a man again. "You Germans. Always a drama."

"You are a policeman. It would be easily arranged."

"And would it satisfy your conscience for 'Canned Goods'? Your life is no good to me. Yes, I thought the trials at Nürnberg a farce. I would have shot them right away. 'While trying to escape'—the classic formula. But I can't shoot you."

"You are going to let me go? To die my lingering little death, reading the Bible every day?"

"I have to decide."

"What do you believe?" Müller asked suddenly.

"Do not ask me what I believe."

"I am a better policeman than you are, Mr. Van der Valk."

"Perhaps," Van der Valk said. "We shall see."

Fear suddenly went over the face again, despite the self-control.

"You are going to arrest me."

"That is my duty."

The hand went suddenly to the pistol, but the degenerated nerves were too unsure. Van der Valk released the grip, put the catch on, and stuck the thing in his pocket.

"Put your overcoat on."

"You're going to give me to the Jews."

"I'm going to give you to the government of the Kingdom of the Netherlands. No Jews will kidnap you."

"I see no difference," bitterly. "You take refuge

under your official identity—I thought you were a
man. Your Kingdom will do the same. Officially,
praiseworthily, they will give me to the Jews. You.
Bureaucrat. Without the courage either to let me go or
to shoot me."

"Listen to me." Van der Valk's voice, he could
hear, was not under control. "Every instinct I have is
to let you go. Moral, ethical, legal, personal—call it
what you like; I don't care. And it would be ex-
pedient into the bargain. I won't do it."

He watched Müller bring his features under control.

"Very well," said the old voice, with its calm, quiet
tone. "I had all the same reasons to surrender myself
—and I could not do that, either. You are right to
force me." It had dignity. For the first time, Van der
Valk felt his old liking, even respect, for the man.

"I will get my coat." Müller turned to him again.
"I have courage, you know."

They walked, the old man using his rubber-tipped
stick. They passed the Jewish cemetery. Müller glanced
up at the Hebrew characters on the gateposts. "You
know what it says?"

"I can't read Hebrew."

"I can," softly. "One of Müller's strange accom-
plishments. It says, 'Born, mankind is doomed to die.
Dead, mankind is destined to live again.' "

They walked on.

"Grace," suddenly. "Oliver Cromwell fought his
hardest battles for it. A crowning mercy."

"I don't believe," Van der Valk said, "that grace
has to be fought for. I believe it's there for the asking."

They reached the police bureau. The desk man rec-

ognized Van der Valk this time; he got up. Seeing Besançon, he looked puzzled. Then what had they
arrested Miss Burger for?

"This man is to be given a cell. I want him treated
with every consideration. There's no charge, at present."

"But what am I to put on the form, Inspector?"

"Oh, some stupid bureaucratic phrase. 'Provisional
detention pending judicial decision.' Never mind, I'll
do it. Here, give me the keys."

The fellow looked bemused, but wasn't going to
question an officer. Van der Valk opened the steel
door. The bureau was a modern one, and the cell
was clean and well kept.

"Say nothing here—you understand. I'll see about
changing this as soon as I possibly can. In the mean-
time, you'll be brought everything you need from
your home."

The old man was trembling badly, shakier than
Van der Valk had ever seen him. But the eyes—the
faamous darting eyes of legend—were steady. He
looked very resolute.

"Thank you."

Van der Valk turned back abruptly at the door.
"Forgive me." He held out his hand.

"You are willing to shake hands with Heinrich Müller?"

"Yes."

Müller pulled himself up, and gave Van der Valk a
formal German bow.

"I'll phone your inspector," Van der Valk said to
the desk man, who was fussing about Christian

Names and Date and Place of Birth. "No—I'd better go around to his house."

"Safety of the Realm Act?"

"I've no idea myself. If I were you, I'd say and do nothing till you hear. I'll make a personal report to the Procureur-Général tomorrow morning. He'll decide."

"But, my God, Van der Valk—who is it?"

"S.S. Lieutenant General Heinrich Müller."

It made a good exit line.

7

"Inspector Van der Valk, Central Recherche, requests an interview with Mr. Sailer."

"You mean this morning?"

"It is extremely urgent. I can't put that strongly enough."

"I'll see what I can do," rather astonished. "Will you wait?"

"Yes."

"Mr. Sailer will see you now."

"Ah, Van der Valk. Good morning. This is rather unusual. I take it a request of this sort is not made without grave reason?"

"Very grave, sir. I need your advice, and I need your help."

"You have committed an imprudence?"

"No, sir. But I have done something from which I shall never be quite free."

"Connected with this affair in Drente?"

"There are two affairs, sir. The first was simple—I have a report for you here, which I would have sent over by messenger this morning. But the other—"

"A grave affair?"

"Yes. And a headline—in every newspaper in the world."

"I am at your service. That, among other things, is what I am here for."

"At its briefest—I have, while in Drente, discovered, identified, and arrested Gestapo Müller. He's in detention—no charge on the form, and under his assumed name—in the local bureau. I have notified the local inspector—he didn't know what to do any more than I did. He agreed to wait until I had made a verbal report."

Mr. Sailer considered, in silence, Van der Valk's rather hysterical words. "Nobody, Van der Valk, need envy an incumbent of this chair. Very well. You had better relate me your story in detail."

". . . And for these reasons, and the fact that I know I am not altogether fitted for my responsibilities, I would like to offer my resignation. That's all, sir."

There was a very long silence. Mr. Sailer's head was upright, but his eyes rested on his hands, which were folded upon his blotter. He raised them slowly; they stayed on Van der Valk, who tried to meet them the way Müller had met his.

"Nothing can alter the course of the law," very quietly.

"I can't argue with you, sir. I certainly can't query a a judicial opinion of yours. But if I'm no longer a policeman, I could say that the law makes no provision

for a man like that. As a man—even as a policeman
—I can say that no man expiates crimes like that.
Any way at all. It's something needed from the whole
human race."

"Go on." But Van der Valk had lost his grip on himself.

"I can't help it. He's only a man. Not only because
I talked to him, shook hands with him, liked him. Ach,
I'm no good for this job. He said to himself—a fellow
that knows something about policemen."

"That'll do."

There was another long pause. Mr. Sailer was making up his mind.

"You have earned respect by what you have done.
And, personally, I admire you.

"A bad policeman—you will please allow your superiors to judge of that. Mr. Müller's superiors"—in
the voice like desert sand for which Sailer was known
—"appear to have found him useful, but we would
not—nor, I think, would they—recommend him as a
textbook model.

"Your responsibility does not reach as far as a case
that, as you pointed out, has not been imagined, for
which no provision has been made in the Criminal
Code, for which there are no precedents in jurisprudence. Your conscience is not an official concern, nor
is it mine. You have behaved with scrupulous exacti-
tude in acting as you have and in making—shall I
call it a confession?—to me. I approve your movements unhesitatingly.

"The responsibility is now mine. You may have a
confidence in exchange for your own; I will endeavor
to apply moral principles to my decision in this matter

—as you did. The matter is from this moment out of your hands."

Another pause, shorter.

"Your resignation is refused. The State of the Netherlands, embodied at this instant in myself, will not accept the loss of a responsible public servant for the motives you have given me."

Mr. Sailer leaned forward slightly. His small healthy eyes impaled Van der Valk. "I will recommend your promotion within a short term. In particular, your transfer to a department where, I think, your qualities will find use. I am thinking of the juvenile branch.

"Lastly, I have, this morning, received a letter from the burgomaster of Zwinderen. He speaks of you in high terms, and sees fit to inform me that you were of personal service to himself in a situation placing a public official in a difficult position. I have, I think, no more to say. Have you?"

"No, sir."

"I have no doubt but that Mr. Tak has plenty for you to do. You can leave your written report here."

There is in Holland a comic strip. The drawings are good, and the text original, witty, sharp in grasp of character; a comic strip with character—that is very rare. It concerns a very stupid, snobbish, pleasant bear whose name is Olivier B. Bommel. He is a nice fellow, very aristocratic. He lives in a castle called Schloss Bommelstein, where he has a butler who is an excellent cook. And by sacred tradition, a Bommel adventure must always end with a festive, abundant dinner.

Arlette, who tended to exaggerate, said that Bom-

mel was the only readable literature in Holland;
Van der Valk had often been inclined to agree. He
agreed with the tradition, too. When he got home,
quite as stupid and bewildered as Bommel ever is, he
found Arlette had made a very famous country dish:
boiled ham with the four purées—apples, potatoes,
celery, and flageolet beans.

Van der Valk did not tell her he had wanted to resign. Nor anything about General Müller. What would
have been the point? Because he had not slept last
night, should she not be allowed to sleep tonight?

It would have been a waste, too, of a good dinner.
And his free weekend.

"We seem to have got quite an enthusiastic letter
from the burgomaster. And there was a hint that I
may be promoted, after all. There's a vacancy in the
juvenile branch; I've been told it's me—unofficially.
Post has rank of chief inspector. Good, hm?"

"Oh, darling. Where could we go on a holiday
when you get a raise?"

"Anyway, not beautiful Drente, wouldn't you agree?"

"It wasn't that bad," said Arlette. "Looking back,
I'd say I quite enjoyed myself."

ABOUT THE AUTHOR

NICOLAS FREELING was born in London and raised in France and England. After his military service in World War II, he traveled extensively throughout Europe, working as a professional cook in a number of hotels and restaurants. His first book, *Love in Amsterdam*, was published in 1961. Since then, he has written seventeen novels and two non-fiction works. His most recent books have been *Gadget*, a novel of suspense, and the third Henri Castang novel, *Sabine*. Mr. Freeling was awarded a golden dagger by the Crime Writers in 1963, the Grand Prix de Roman Policier in 1965, and the Edgar Allen Poe Award of the Mystery Writers Association in 1966.

Mr. Freeling lives in France with his wife and their five children.